MW01133132

HIGHLAND SPIRIT

HIGHLAND CHRONICLES SERIES - BOOK 2

ELIZABETH ROSE

ROSESCRIBE MEDIA INC.

Copyright © 2019 by Elizabeth Rose Krejcik

This is a work of fiction. All characters, names, places and incidents are either
a product of the author's imagination or used fictitiously. Any similarity to
actual organizations or persons living or deceased is entirely coincidental. All
rights reserved. No part of this book may be used, reproduced or transmitted
in any form whatsoever without the author's written permission.

Cover created by Elizabeth Rose Krejcik
Edited by Scott Moreland

ISBN: 978-1672848640

AUTHOR'S NOTE

Since my stories span the generations, I am listing a quick family tree for the entire series so you can use it as a reference guide when reading the books. To find a more in-depth family tree, including brothers and sisters of my heroes, please visit my website at **http://elizabethrosenovels.com**.

Cast of Characters – Family Tree:

(Highland Spirit features the hero, Ethan MacKeefe, and the heroine, Alana Chisholm)

Hawke MacKeefe: Book 1

Callum MacKeefe (Hawke's great-grandfather)

  Ian MacKeefe (Callum's son and Hawke's grandfather – MacKeefe Clan Chieftain)

  Lady Clarista (Ian's English wife and Hawke's grandmother)

Storm MacKeefe (Ian's son and Hawke's father – also MacKeefe Clan Chieftain)
    Lady Wren (Storm's English wife, and Hawke's mother)
    Hawke MacKeefe (Storm and Wren's son)

Ethan MacKeefe: Book 2

Onyx MacKeefe (One of the Madmen MacKeefe and Ethan's father)
    Lady Lovelle (Ethan's stepmother)
    Janneth Chisholm (Ethan's mother)
    Ethan (Janneth and Onyx's illegitimate son)

Caleb MacKeefe: Book 3

Ian MacKeefe (One of the Madmen MacKeefe and Caleb's father – not to be confused with Hawke's grandfather, MacKeefe Clan Chieftain, also named Ian)
    Kyla (Caleb's mother and also Aidan MacKeefe's sister)
    Caleb (Ian and Kyla's son)

Logan MacKeefe: Book 4

Aidan MacKeefe (One of the Madmen MacKeefe and Logan's father)
    Effie MacDuff (Logan's mother)
    Logan (Aidan and Effie's son)

"Yer uncle is dead, yer mathair has been abducted, and yer faither is bein' hunted by his own clan."

Alana Chisholm froze, not able to believe the message that her father's friend, Albert, just whispered in her ear. In a few minutes' time she'd be marrying her childhood sweetheart, Ethan MacKeefe, and this news was the last thing she wanted to hear right now. She'd been waiting for her family to arrive for the wedding but never expected this.

"Nay, say it isna so, Albert," she whispered back to the man, glancing over her shoulder at the members of the MacKeefe Clan who were not privy to her father's immoral habits. The MacKeefes were already celebrating although she and Ethan had yet to say their vows. The entire camp had been busy all morning preparing food for the celebration, getting ready to welcome Alana into their clan as Ethan's wife.

Ethan waited near the archway of flowers, jesting with his good friends, Hawke, Logan, and Caleb. He looked so handsome in his saffron leine and purple and green plaid that were the colors of the MacKeefe Clan. The priest conversed with Storm MacKeefe, the laird of the clan. Old Callum MacKeefe was already passing out the Mountain Magic – his potent brew of whisky. Everyone was here except for Alana's parents.

The MacKeefes stalled while they waited for her family. Today, she was supposed to become wife to the man she loved. This wedding was crucial since Alana had a secret that she'd not shared with anyone – not even Ethan. "Please dinna tell me this now, Albert. I'm about to get married!"

If this message was coming to her now, it could only mean one thing. Her family truly needed her. And she had to try to help them. Her body became numb at the news of her uncle's death. Fear coursed through her to learn that her mother had been abducted. This all had to do with her father's little problem of getting mixed up in things that were less than admirable, she was sure of it. If it wasn't his gambling, it was his drinking or fighting, or something else that always landed him in trouble. If it weren't for Alana usually being able to smooth things over for him, her father would probably be dead by now. Alana had a knack for making things right. Give her a bad situation and she was usually able to turn it around and find the good in it. But today, she had the feeling this would not be the case.

Alana's world came crashing down around her and she felt helpless to stop it this time. Laying her hand on her belly she tried her best to still the turmoil and anticipation welling within her. However, it did naught to calm her. She suddenly felt frozen in fear to think that she might not get to marry Ethan after all. She'd waited too long and she didn't want anything to stop this wedding from happening.

"We've got to go, Alana," Albert told her with urgency in his voice. "Yer faither is waitin' for us at the shore. He's got a friend with a boat. Kirstine and Finn are already in the cart ready to go."

She noticed her younger sister and brother who had been here helping her prepare for her wedding now sitting in a wagon hidden behind some brush. The horse pulling the wagon neighed and snorted as if it were irritated as well. Albert knew all her father's bad vices but was still his friend. So were a few others of the clan that her father trusted. These men now waited on horseback next to the wagon, ready to take her away.

"B-but, surely this can wait. Please," she begged him. Her heart about beat from her chest and she felt like she was going to swoon. Turning back to see the MacKeefes across camp laughing and talking, her eyes settled on Ethan's tall, dark, and handsome form. She'd waited so long for this day. She was already eight and ten years of age and still not married like most of the rest of the girls in her clan. She'd known Ethan her entire life and only had eyes for him. They belonged together. "Today is my weddin' day, Albert!" she said, her bottom lip trembling. Her knees quaked as anxiety grew within her.

Alana couldn't deny a request from her father. He counted on her more than anyone, ever since her mother threatened to leave him because of his ill-conceived ways. Alana had to be there for him. She couldn't let him down. But neither could she walk away before she'd married Ethan. They'd planned a future together and she would not be the one to take that away from him.

"I canna go," she cried.

"Ye must! Now, let's move quickly. Yer faither awaits us at the docks with a ship ready to sail to Ireland."

"Ireland?" she asked, just as surprised to hear this as the rest of the news. "But our home is in Scotland."

"No' anymore, it isna, lassie," the man told her with a frown. "I'm afraid yer faither is considered a fugitive now. He's done some very bad things. He's a wanted man by more than one clan. A group of those he's wronged are headed this way to find him as we speak. Anyone related or tied to him in any way is in danger. Ye must come with us for yer own safety and ye canna tell a soul. It is yer faither's orders."

"Nay! I'll be safe here with the MacKeefes," she told him. "Ethan will protect me once I'm his wife."

"I'm afraid that might no' be true," he said sadly. "Ye see, while the MacKeefes were preparin' for yer weddin', yer faither has stolen their livestock from the hills and tried to sell it to the MacDougals. However, the MacDougals were no' so easily fooled. All hell is about to break loose. Once the MacKeefes find out what happened, they'll want yer faither's head like everyone else." Albert took her by the arm and pulled her along with him. The bouquet of flowers she'd been holding dropped to the ground. Hurrying along, she almost tripped on her long skirt as they made their way over the rocky ground to the wagon.

"Wait," she said, breaking free of the man's hold. "I need to say somethin' to Ethan before I go. I need to let him ken I still want to marry him. I have to tell him when I'll be back. When will we return?"

"Lass, Ethan will no' want ye after this. And I'm no' sure we'll ever be back," said Albert shaking his head.

"Never?" she asked in astonishment. "Well, then I'm no' goin' with ye! I'm sure Ethan will understand I had nothin' to do with this." Once again, she laid her hand on her belly, rubbing it in small circles, lost in thought. "My place is here with Ethan."

"Ye're wrong! Yer family needs ye now more than ever, Alana. Do no' leave them at a time like this. It is important that yer family stays together no matter what happens. Ye have always been the one to keep them together, so dinna desert them in their time of need. Ye need to help find a way to free yer mathair."

"What can I possibly do?" she asked, not wanting to leave Ethan but also not wanting to abandon her family, especially her mother, at a time like this. To think someone might be hurting her mother or treating her like a prisoner made Alana very angry, indeed. The weight of the world was on her shoulders now. Her family depended on her for her strength. She was damned if she did and damned if she didn't. No matter what choice she made, she would lose someone she loved before this day was over.

"Alana, hurry!" called out Kirstine, her sixteen-year-old sister from the cart. She clutched their eight-year-old brother, Finn to her chest in a protective manner. "There are men approachin' on horseback and they look angry."

"Losh me! It's the MacDougals," said Albert, looking up over Alana's head. "They got here faster than I thought. We need to leave at once!" He turned to go but stopped and looked back at Alana when he realized she didn't follow. "What is yer decision, lass? What shall I tell yer faither? He canna do this without yer help. Ye ken he is a weak-willed man and always looks to ye as his savior."

Alana had to make a choice quickly. But whatever she decided, she was sure she would someday regret it in the end.

With her mother's life at stake and her father running for his life, there was nothing else Alana could do. She had to protect her siblings and help her family. Maybe together they could figure out a way to free her mother and clear her father's name. But to do that she'd need a miracle. If all that Albert told her was true, and if she stayed behind, it could possibly mean she'd never see her family again.

"I will come with ye," said Alana softly, her heart already breaking by her choice. "Guidbye, Ethan," she whispered, looking back at him with tears in her eyes as she headed for the wagon. A group of angry Scots rode into the MacKeefe camp shouting and chaos broke out. Holding her hand over her belly, there was only one thing that would comfort her now. Even though she had to leave the man she loved, a part of him would stay with her forever because she was pregnant with Ethan MacKeefe's baby.

They made it to the shore quickly, racing to the small trade ship preparing to leave. They'd all climbed aboard but what Alana saw made the blood freeze in her veins.

"Papa? she asked, seeing her father bound and gagged, tied to the center pole. Her mother lay in a heap at his feet. "Mathair," screamed Alana, running and dropping to her knees, leaning over the woman and screaming to see her bruised and bleeding body. "Why did they do this to ye?" she cried, not understanding any of this at all.

"Alana," her mother whispered, pushing up to her knees. Alana put her arm around the woman and leaned over to hear her soft voice. It seemed to take most of her mother's strength just to speak. "Yer uncle died to protect the secret. So will I, if need be."

"What?" asked Alana, thinking she'd heard her mother wrong, bending closer to her so she wouldn't miss a word. "Forgive yer faither, and protect yer siblin's when I'm gone."

"Blethers, Mathair, what do ye mean? What is goin' on?"

"Welcome to hell, lassie," came a low voice and chuckle, causing her to turn her head. A dark-haired man about twenty years her senior walked down the pier and boarded the boat. He was followed by a few other men. "Set sail, quickly," he told his crew before turning back to Alana. "My name is Diarmad and ye are all now my prisoners."

Alana's heart sank as the ship set out to sea with them on it.

"Who are ye and why are ye doin' this?" she screamed at the man, cradling her mother's head on her lap. She heard Kirstine and Finn crying behind her.

"Yer faither trusted the wrong man, and then he crossed me. But now that I've got ye all together, one of ye can tell me where to find the treasure. If no', ye'll all end up dead like yer uncle, or beaten like yer mathair."

Alana recognized Diarmad now. He was a man her father brought to live with the clan recently. She always felt he was no good and now this proved it. Diarmad's men surrounded them, providing no means of escape.

"I dinna ken about any treasure," she told him.

"Alana, if ye ken where yer uncle hid the Templar treasure, tell them," her father urged her in his slurred speech. He was either soused again, or possibly near dead.

"Nay! Never tell them," said her mother, Gavina. She held

7

on to the bulkhead of the ship and got to her feet, looking as if she barely had the strength to stand. "Alana, we must keep it safe."

"But Mathair, I dinna ken where any treasure is hidden." She snuck a glance at Diarmad from the corners of her eyes. She'd known her mother and her Uncle Freddie used to whisper about keeping a treasure safe until someone came to get it. But she never understood what it was all about.

"I'm dyin', Alana. Come give me a hug and a kiss guidbye." Her mother held one hand under her cloak and reached out to Alana with the other.

"Nay! Dinna die, Mathair. I need ye." Tears dripped down her cheeks and she moved closer to her. "Mathair, I am pregnant with Ethan MacKeefe's baby."

"What?" growled her father. "How could ye do such a fool thing?"

"I'm happy for ye," said her mother, reaching out and taking Alana's hand in hers. "Ethan MacKeefe is a guid man. He can help ye . . . find the answers."

"Enough!" commanded Diarmad, moving toward them as the ship got farther from the shore. "Now someone better tell me where that treasure is, because I'm no' releasin' any of ye until I get what I want."

"I am the only one who kens where it is," said her mother. "My husband and children ken naught about it."

Alana kissed and hugged her mother, and when she did, her mother slipped something into her hand and whispered in her ear. "It is all up to ye now, Daughter. Never give up. Find the madman. He will help ye."

Alana looked down to see a small metal key in her hand with a Templar cross engraved in the middle. She quickly hid it from Diarmad, dropping it into her pocket. She was about to ask her mother what she meant, when her mother pulled a hidden dagger out of her cloak. She pushed Alana aside and lunged at Diarmad.

"Nay!" cried Alana as she stumbled and fell to the ground. She watched in horror as her mother tried to kill the evil man. But a guard jumped in front of him with his sword drawn and stabbed her mother right through the heart.

"Mathair!" screamed Alana, frozen in fear. Her mother's hand opened and the dagger hit the wooden deck. Then her knees buckled beneath her and she fell to the ground at Diarmad's feet. "Nay!" shouted Alana, getting up and trying to run to her, but another man held her back. Kirstine and Finn held each other, watching in horror and crying.

"She's dead," announced the guard, pulling his sword out of her mother's chest. "I saved yer life, Diarmad," he said proudly.

"Ye fool!" shouted Diarmad. "She was our last hope of ever findin' that treasure. I didna want her dead! Ye'll pay for this." In anger, Diarmad drew his sword and killed the guard. The man's body crumpled in a heap, falling atop her mother.

"Get them out of here," commanded Diarmad as it started to rain. He sheathed his sword and walked over to Alana. Alana struggled against the man who held her.

"Yer mathair said somethin' to ye about the treasure, didna she?" he asked. "Tell me. Where is it?"

"I wouldna tell ye even if I kent!" she spat.

He reached out and slapped her across the face. Alana had been numb because of what she'd just witnessed, but the pain made her feel the anger welling within her, making her feel alive again.

"Ye killed my wife!" shouted her father, pulling at the ropes that bound him. "I'll kill ye for this, Diarmad, I swear I will."

"Nay, ye're wrong." Diarmad turned to look at her father. "I didna kill her and neither would I have. It was the foolish mistake of my guard. And as ye see, he's paid for it with his life. And before ye accuse me of killin' yer brother-by-marriage, his death was an accident when he fell and hit his head tryin' to flee."

"Release me. And let my family go." Alana's father pulled at the ropes so hard his wrists began to bleed.

"Ye're no' goin' anywhere, Chisholm," growled Diarmad. "I've set ye up so that no clan will ever want ye near them again. They all want to kill ye because of things ye've done. Ye have nowhere to go now and neither does yer family. Ye'll stay with me. Ye'll all be my family now."

"Nay! Never. I never should have listened to ye," yelled her father.

"Nay, ye shouldna. That was yer first mistake." Diarmad chuckled. "Ye were an easy mark, but I never expected yer brother-by-marriage to die, nor yer wife to put up a fight. This treasure must be worth more than I thought. I will no' set any of ye free until ye hand it over."

"We dinna ken about any treasure," shouted Alana. "Let us go."

"Och, that's a lie, lassie," snarled Diarmad. "After all, yer faither was the one to tell me about it in the first place or I'd never have kent about it at all. Isna that so, Chisholm?"

"Faither?" whispered Alana, shaking her head as her father's face turned sullen and he looked to the ground.

"I'm sorry, Alana. I didna mean to do it. But Diarmad made

me believe we'd all be rich from it and that I could use it to pay off my debts."

"Yer faither is weak, but I see ye are strong like yer mathair." Diarmad reached out and ran a finger along Alana's cheek, making her cringe. "To make certain none of ye will try to leave me, I'm goin' to take ye as my wife."

"What? Nay!" she cried, panicked to think she'd be marrying him today instead of Ethan. "I canna marry ye and I would never! I am Ethan MacKeefe's betrothed and I am carryin' his bairn. He'll hunt ye down like a dog to find me and then he'll skin ye alive."

Diarmad made a tisking sound with his tongue. "No' true," he said. "Ye see, yer betrothed's clan thinks ye betrayed them now. Besides, my man, Fergus, killed Ethan just before we boarded the boat. Of course, it was in self-defense."

"Nay!" she cried, not wanting to believe it. Emotions swept through her. "I dinna believe ye. Ye lie!"

"Fergus, tell her it's the truth," said Diarmad.

"Diarmad, I need to talk with ye," said the man, calling Diarmad over to him. They conversed in secret for a minute and then Alana saw Fergus hand something to his leader. Diarmad looked angry at first, but then he smiled and headed back to Alana as the ship continued to sail and Scotland got further and further away.

"Here's all the proof ye need." Diarmad held out his open palm. Alana looked down to see a bloodied piece of the MacKeefe plaid. Atop it sat the wedding ring that Ethan was going to put on her finger at the ceremony.

"Nay, that's no' my ring," she said in denial, shaking her head.

"Take it, lass. Look at it closely and ye'll see that it is."

With two fingers Alana picked up the ring and inspected it. Inside the gold circle were engraved their names – Alana and Ethan. She clutched the ring, holding it to her chest, feeling her heart breaking when she realized Ethan was dead. Too angry to cry, too shaken to try to fight the man, a lone tear dripped down her cheek.

"No need to keep that, since ye willna be marryin' him after all," said Diarmad, ripping the ring from her hand.

"Nay! My ring!" she cried, not wanting to lose one of the last remembrances she had of Ethan. "Isna it enough ye've already killed Ethan, my mathair and my uncle? Please, at least let me keep the ring. Ye've taken everythin' else."

Diarmad looked at the ring in his hand, his eyes slowly lifting to meet hers. "I told ye – I didna kill any of them. Keep the blamed thing, I dinna care!" He threw it to the ground at her feet. Alana dropped to her knees and scooped it up, bringing it to her mouth in a kiss.

"I think I changed my mind about ye," said Diarmad, thumping his fingers against his cheek in thought. "Ye are too much trouble. Besides, I dinna want a wench who is already deflowered and carryin' a dead man's bastard as my wife."

Alana felt relief push through her pain, until she heard what Diarmad said next.

"I'll marry yer sister, instead. Kirstine, is it? She'll give me bairns and ye'll all be part of my family now so there will be no need to ever try to leave."

"Nay!" screamed Alana, fearing for her sister. "Do no' touch Kirstine."

"Bring the girl to me," Diarmad instructed his men.

"Alana, help me!" cried Kirstine as the guard pulled her

and Finn apart. She was young and innocent, and very frightened.

"Leave her be!" Alana ran to her sister, gathering her into her arms in a protective hold.

"Tell me where the treasure is, and mayhap I'll no' marry yer sister after all," Diarmad tried to bargain.

"I dinna ken," cried Alana, really not knowing. "Honest, I dinna ken at all."

"Throw them in the hold!" commanded Diarmad, storming away to the forecastle of the ship. "When we get to Ireland, I'll marry the lass. And one way or another, I will find that treasure no matter how long it takes. I'll find it if it's the last thing I ever do."

"Alana, I'm scared," whimpered Kirstine, clinging to her.

"Me, too," said Finn, running to them as Alana gathered them both into her arms.

"Dinna worry," she said, gripping her wedding ring tightly, horrified, sad and angry because she would never see the man she loved again. Then she thought of the key her mother gave her that was hidden in her pocket. Her hand slid down to cover it from outside her clothes. If Diarmad had known she had it, he would surely have taken it as well. "I will somehow find that treasure. I'll find it and we'll trade it for our lives."

Alana only had her mother's last words and the mysterious key to go by, but she had to figure it out. Their lives depended on it now.

She tried to comfort her brother and sister, and tried not to think of Ethan or she'd break down crying. She had to be strong. For her sister and brother. But her mother's last warning to protect the treasure at all costs echoed in her mind. Her mother died to keep the treasure out of the wrong hands. Her uncle was dead because of it, too. Alana's hand caressed her belly as the guards led them past her father and to the hold. She realized she had to do whatever it took to help her family . . . and to protect Ethan's unborn baby.

The weight of the world was on her shoulders again, but this time it felt too heavy to bear.

CHAPTER 1

FIVE YEARS LATER SCOTLAND, 1385

*E*than MacKeefe was known throughout the land as being a rugged, mighty Highland warrior, excellent with a sword, a beast during battle, and afraid of nothing . . . except for mayhap ghosts.

"Come on, Ethan. What are ye doin' just sittin' there?" complained Ethan's good friend, Hawke, jumping to the shore from the boat that they'd just sailed from the mainland to the Isle of Kerrera. The boy named Oliver traveled with them. Hawke held out his hand to help the boy to shore, but Oliver stubbornly pushed it away.

Oliver was nine, and his sister, Sophie, who was back on shore, was six years of age. They were born of Hawke's late wife, Osla, although Hawke was not their father. Since the passing of the children's mother, Hawke and his new wife, Phoebe, took them into their care. Osla had been Phoebe's cousin.

"We need to find Sophie's doll," Hawke reminded Ethan. "Her nonstop cryin' ever since her mathair passed away is drivin' the clan mad. Oliver says she probably left it somewhere near the large rock behind the hut where they used to live. I hope we can find it."

"I can find it," said the boy confidently. "And I dinna need ye two to help me do it."

"Listen, lad," said Hawke with a scowl, having no patience anymore. He was used to being a loner, and definitely not comfortable around children yet. "It's nighttime and we're on a remote isle that is said to be haunted. No' to mention, ye are naught but a lad. Ye'll take our help and like it."

"Nay," protested the boy. "I dinna care what ye say. I'm no' afraid. I dinna need anyone." Oliver took off at a sprint into the darkness, causing Hawke to release a frustrated breath. His hands balled up into fists before he slowly released them.

"Are ye comin' with us, Ethan?" asked Hawke, looking back over his shoulder. "Or are ye goin' to sit there starin' up at that bluidy castle all night long?"

"Everyone kens about Blackbriar Castle," said Ethan, being very superstitious and wanting to go nowhere near it. "It is cursed and we shouldna be here."

"God's bones, Ethan, ever since Alana betrayed and left ye, I swear ye've been actin' like a dolt. In the past five years, ye've become even more superstitious than ever. It's ridiculous that ye still fear imaginary ghosts although ye're a man of six and twenty years."

Ethan never did get over the fact that his betrothed played him for a fool, working alongside her thieving father to betray him. He'd been in love with the girl and thought she loved him, too. But when he realized their wedding was naught but part of a ploy to steal the MacKeefe cattle, he was heartbroken as well as furious. One of the clan members saw Alana willingly leave the MacKeefe camp the day of the wedding with a man. It was just before the MacDougals arrived to tell them what happened. She'd boarded a ship with her entire family and sailed away, never to be seen again. He was almost glad when he found out Caleb's pine marten stole the wedding ring, because he would never be able to look at it again without feeling like his life was ruined.

"The ghosts are no' imaginary," said Ethan, speaking of not only the ghost of Blackbriar Castle but also the ghosts of his past.

Ethan was a brave man, but this isle truly spooked him. As a boy, he once took up the challenge from his friends of coming here and also entering the castle on his own. He'd taken the dare because he liked a challenge and was mischievous in many ways. He lived with the Chisholms then, since his mother belonged to the clan. It was many years later, on his mother's deathbed, when he discovered his father was Onyx MacKeefe. After her passing, he found his father and moved to the MacKeefe Clan instead.

As a boy, he'd seen a ghost the night he entered Blackbriar Castle and, to this day it still spooked him. The worst part was that his friends never believed him and he'd ended up being teased about it his entire life.

"Ye ken the stories as well as anyone," Ethan told Hawke. "And dinna forget we both heard the ghost scream the last time we were here." It was said a crazy old man that everyone called Mad Murdock lived in the ruins of the old castle by himself. The story was that he murdered his bride and tossed her out the tower window on their wedding night. "I saw the ghost of Mad Murdock's bride when I was a child, Hawke," continued Ethan. "People still hear her scream all the time, all the way to the mainland sometimes. She walks the battlements to this day lookin' to get revenge on her husband."

"Blethers!" said Hawke, waving his hand through the air. "It's all idle gossip, Ethan, and ye ken it. Ye canna believe everythin' ye hear. No matter what ye thought ye saw, ye were mistaken. After all, yer faither was at one time thought to be a demon because of his two different-colored eyes, but we all ken it is no' true."

"Then what about the screams?" asked Ethan. "Ye canna deny ye heard them, too."

"It was probably only a night owl or a wolf. It certainly wasna a ghost."

Running a hand over his wolfhound's back in thought, Ethan looked up at the dark, dreary castle in the distance illuminated only by the light of the moon. Tangled vines and dead trees surrounded the crumbling walls. He felt a chill run up his spine and it wasn't just because of the weather. Someone was watching them. He could feel it in his bones. And he didn't like it one bit. All he wanted to do was to turn around and sail back to the MacKeefe camp on the mainland. A warm fire and a potent tankard of Old Callum MacKeefe's Mountain Magic was what he really needed right now.

The night was dark and the air was chilly this eve. A fine dusting of fresh snow covered the ground. He stared at the brooding castle on the cliffs above him and pulled his cloak closer for warmth. Blackbriar Castle was thought to be abandoned now, since no one had seen Mad Murdock on the mainland in years. Bards told stories that the ghost of the wife of Murdock killed him and that he was lying dead somewhere inside the ruins. They also said that anyone who dared to attempt to enter the castle wound up cursed or dead. It was an evil place and because of it, no one stepped foot on this isle if they didn't have to.

Without a doubt, Ethan knew it was a mistake to come here, especially at night and in a storm.

"For the love of God, Ethan, move yer bluidy arse!" growled Hawke. "I dinna have time to hold yer hand while ye worry like a wench. I need to go after the lad before he gets lost or mayhap hurt. I promised Phoebe I'd watch after him and now he's gone and run off on me."

"Stop it, Hawke," snarled Ethan, not liking the way his friend talked to him. "And remember, Oliver lived on this isle his entire life even if it was against his will. I am sure he could walk it in his sleep and still no' get lost. So ye are the one who is worryin' like a wench, no' me."

"Och, mayhap so," agreed Hawke, running a weary hand through his hair. "But I dinna like the idea of the boy takin' off in the dark by himself. I am responsible for him now. I need to find him quickly. If anythin' happens to him while he's in my care, Phoebe will have my head."

Ethan chuckled. "I think bein' afraid of a wife is worse than fearin' any ghost."

"Just wait until ye're married and ye'll see," mumbled Hawke under his breath.

"Dinna say that," Ethan ground out through gritted teeth. Marriage was a sore subject with him ever since Alana abandoned him at the altar and left him for another man. He was so scarred by being betrayed by someone he'd loved that he decided he would never marry in this lifetime. He would never again take the chance of being rejected again because it hurt too much.

"Sorry," said Hawke, realizing what he'd said. "I didna mean anythin' by that."

"I ken," Ethan answered. "So Oliver still doesna like ye, does he?" Ethan stepped from the boat onto the wet shore. In one leap, his large wolfhound made it to the shore as well.

"Nay, he doesna, and I dinna ken what to do to gain his trust." The fact that Oliver rejected Hawke really bothered him now that he was in the position of being the boy's father. It was an odd situation, but both Hawke and the boy needed to accept each other even though it might take some time.

"Mayhap ye should let me help ye," said Ethan with a chuckle. "After all, children like me. They dinna fear me the way they do ye. With yer disposition, I'm sure they all think ye're goin' to bite off their heads."

"Hah!" spat Hawke. "Children are no' afraid of me, and neither are they afraid of a little ol' ghost that doesna even exist. Therefore, I doubt ye'll be of any help to me at all. Now stop all this clishmaclaver and let's go."

Ethan started to follow Hawke back to the hut where Oliver used to live with his mother and sister as nothing more than prisoners of an evil man named Euan who was now thankfully dead. But when his hound, Trapper, started barking at something in the dark, he stopped in his tracks.

"What is it, boy?" Ethan reached out with one hand, running it over the dog's back. With his other hand, he gripped the hilt of his sword tightly. He was on full alert should he need to fight.

"He probably just saw a rat. It's nothin'," Hawke called back as he started out after the boy.

"Aye, that's all it was," Ethan tried to convince himself, but he knew it wasn't so. From the corners of his eyes in the moonlight, he thought he saw a dark figure running toward the castle.

"Did ye see that, Hawke?" asked Ethan with wide eyes, pointing in the opposite direction.

"I canna hear ye, Ethan, and neither will I wait for ye," came Hawke's reply from the dark. "If ye're no' back at the boat when we're ready to leave, ye can stay here on this godforsaken isle by yerself." Hawke's voice drifted off as he hurried away in the opposite direction.

"I'm with ye," said Ethan, turning to follow Hawke. But when Trapper growled lowly and took off at a run in the opposite direction, Ethan stopped once again.

"Trapper, come here!" he shouted, but the hound didn't listen. It was on the trail of something and kept heading in the opposite direction until Ethan could barely see it. "Bid the devil," he grumbled, glancing back at the path Hawke had taken and then over to where his dog had gone. There was no doubt in Ethan's mind where the animal was going. Trapper was headed right for the haunted castle. Ethan's stomach clenched and his muscles tightened in his jaw. Then, letting out a deep breath, he turned and started his climb up the hill to the castle – the last place he ever wanted to be.

"Who was it, Finn?" asked Alana Chisholm, meeting her brother in the courtyard of Blackbriar Castle. She'd seen the boat dock at the shore from the tower window and sent the boy out to investigate. No one ever came to the isle, not once in the past year since they'd lived here. That is, no one but a man named Euan to see his family that he'd kept in a hut secluded from everyone else – not unlike the way she and her family lived now. Euan had been part of the smuggling ring that Diarmad now ran since Euan's death.

Alana and her siblings weren't allowed to even speak to the other occupants on the isle or they'd be punished by Diarmad. Then, a few months ago, Osla and her children just up and disappeared.

After birthing her baby in Ireland, Alana continued to play the role of mother to not only her daughter but her siblings as well. Kirstine was married to Diarmad now, and none of them had been able to do anything to stop it. Kirstine birthed him a baby nearly four years ago, but the boy was a stillborn. Since then she'd miscarried twice, but was once again almost ready to birth another baby. Diarmad was insistent on having a son, and would not give up. Alana was thankful he'd never touched her because she was pregnant with Ethan's child. She breathed a sigh of relief but still felt sorry and sickened because her sister had no choice in marrying the evil man.

While Kirstine adapted to her new life as Diarmad's wife, Alana could never accept it. But they were all a part of this life of hell, and could do naught to escape it. Diarmad insisted Alana knew where the secret treasure was hidden and, even after all these years, he wouldn't give up the notion of finding it. Her family would never be truly free of the man until he had it. And even so, Alana wasn't sure if it would even matter anymore. Her father worked with Diarmad running the smuggling ring, and they were all part of this immoral act whether they liked it or not.

Alana had always been the strength of her family, but after

almost dying when she birthed her daughter, Isobel, it had taken her a long time to get her strength back. And even then, she was never the same knowing Ethan had been killed on their wedding day. When that happened, it had taken her will of living from her and she had lost all hope.

But at night when she rocked her daughter to sleep, she somehow felt as if Ethan were still there with her and this was her only comforting thought that got her through each day.

She still had the ring as well as the key her mother had given her the day she'd died. Alana had dismissed any thought of finding the treasure through the years, honestly not knowing where it could be. But lately, she'd been remembering more and more about the bedtime stories her uncle used to tell her when she was a child. They weren't normal stories to comfort a child. Nay, they had to do with a haunted castle and a crazy man named Mad Murdock instead. He'd been talking about Blackbriar Castle on the Isle of Kerrera off the coast of Scotland. Odd, that he chose that to tell her, out of all the stories he could have told.

So when Diarmad decided to move the smuggling ring back to the Isle of Kerrera since it had a hidden cove, she was almost glad. They were back in Scotland again, and this is where her heart longed to be.

Her uncle's bedtime stories about Blackbriar Castle made it sound as if he'd been here. That started her thinking that with its reputation, mayhap the treasure was hidden here. It would be a perfect spot and wouldn't be disturbed. Now, all she had to do was find it and all her prayers would be answered. Perhaps she had a little hope left that someday she and her family could be happy again, and mayhap one day even rejoin their clan.

Their presence here had been kept a secret. They rarely lit torches outside, and the sheep they raised that were stolen and smuggled in were usually kept in a barn that looked abandoned. They were prisoners of Diarmad, even though they were now his family. It was an ill jest of fate that their lives had turned out this way. Her father's health had been failing lately. Still, Diarmad made him work with him at smuggling goods in and out of England, saying he needed to pay back his debt to him, though she knew it could never be repaid. One bad deed done by her father only led to more, she realized. He no longer questioned Diarmad, but just did as he instructed. When had this gotten so out of hand?

Gossip had it that there was once a laird of Blackbriar Castle who lived here and had gone mad. He murdered his bride on their wedding day and threw her out the tower window. Whether or not this really happened, she couldn't be sure. The stories were legends now, and never diminished even after all these years.

To protect their secret, Diarmad made sure the legend lived on to keep outsiders far away. He forced Alana to scream and throw a dummy dressed like a ghost out the window to scare away any intruders or people even thinking about visiting the isle.

"Alana, I saw a boy and two big men in a boat," said her brother. Finn was tall now with blond hair and had a lithe frame. He'd just turned three and ten years of age recently. Her sister, Kirstine, was one and twenty years of age and Alana was three and twenty.

"What boy?" she asked. "Do you mean Oliver, the boy who used to live on the island?" Alana asked anxiously, thinking that the children might have been killed when they disappeared.

"Aye, I'm sure it was him," said Finn. "And the two men on the boat are wearin' plaids. I think they're Highlanders."

"Really." This interested Alana. She hadn't had contact with anyone except for the English smugglers who brought the deliveries to them in secret, docking their ship on the far side of the isle in a hidden cove. She longed to see or perhaps talk to a Highlander again that had naught to do with Diarmad and the others. "What do ye think they want?" she wondered.

"I'm no' sure. I thought I heard them say they were lookin' for somethin' that was left here."

Alana feared for the men's lives. She wasn't sure what Diarmad would do if they wandered closer to the castle. "Mayhap they'll find what they came for and leave quickly."

"Mayhap," said the boy, trying to catch his breath. He sounded as if he had run all the way back from the shore. "But the big, burly Highlander has a hound. I couldna see his face but I'm sure he is mean. The dog followed me up here and is probably right behind me."

"A hound?" she asked.

"It was huge! I think it was a wolfhound."

"By the rood, we've got to close the gate!" she cried. "Fast, Finn, run up to the battlements and tell the guards to lower the gate and raise the drawbridge anon. If they enter the castle, Diarmad will most likely kill them." This was her only way of protecting the strangers, whoever they were.

"I will," he said, taking off at a run.

"Everyone, get inside," Alana shouted, sending the occupants of the castle scurrying about. There weren't many people living at Blackbriar. Diarmad had about a dozen men and a handful of servants. Of course, her family and her father's friends, Albert and Graeme, who had been captured with them now worked for Diarmad as well.

"Alana, what is it?" Her sister, Kirstine, ran up, pulling her cloak tighter around her body. She was carrying her baby low now, and the birth could happen at any time. The wind picked up, making a light flurry of snow swirl around them.

"Strangers are on the isle," Alana reported. "I've instructed Finn to tell the guards to close the gate and raise the drawbridge immediately for their own protection. Where are Diarmad and his men?"

"They're down at the cove, preparin' for the next shipment."

"Guid. Hopefully, the intruders will leave before Diarmad ever sees them."

"Look!" Kirstine's eyes opened wide and she pointed to a large wolfhound that ran right under the descending gate and entered the courtyard. In the light of a few dimly burning torches, Alana saw the terrifying, large beast as it headed right for her.

"Nay!" She held out her hands and turned her head as the dog leapt up and knocked her to the ground. She was sure it was going to bite her or perhaps tear her to shreds. But instead, the hound started licking her face.

She pulled back, looking at the huge white dog that seemed to know her. She had a feeling she knew it, too.

"Trapper?" she said, running a hand over the dog's head, not believing her eyes.

"Whose dog is it?" asked Kirstine curiously.

"It belongs to the Highlanders who docked on the isle,"

said Alana, getting to her feet. "Kirstine, I think this is Ethan's dog."

"Oh," she said, perusing it. "It must belong to another of his clan now since his death."

"Should we kill it?" asked Graeme, calling down from the battlements, always ready to use his sword.

"Nay, it's just a dog," she answered. "Try to catch it and put it outside the gate. Everyone get inside the keep. Kirstine, where is Isobel?" Alana looked around for her four-year-old daughter but didn't see her anywhere.

"I dinna ken," said Kirstine. "She was here just a moment ago."

"I want ye to find her quickly." Alana started away.

"Where are ye goin'?" asked Kirstine.

"I think it's time I do somethin' to scare those Highlanders away before Diarmad kills them."

"I understand," said her sister with a nod. "I'll find Isobel and keep her in the great hall until ye are finished."

* * *

"OPEN THE GATE," shouted Ethan, sure he'd seen Trapper run under the gate and into the castle's courtyard when he approached. It shocked him that the castle seemed to be occupied when he was sure it was abandoned. But when he saw two guards up on the wallwalk, he realized he'd been mistaken.

"Nay! Go away," shouted the guard atop the battlements. "No strangers are allowed in Blackbriar Castle."

"I'm only lookin' for my hound," he told them. "I'm sure he

went inside. Now, I'll tell ye again, open the bluidy gate before I have to knock it down."

The guard chuckled. "Ye just try," he shouted down to Ethan. "If ye ken what's guid for ye, ye'll leave here and never return."

"God's eyes," Ethan mumbled under his breath. All he wanted was to find his dog and leave, but they weren't making it easy for him. He didn't fancy being so close to this wretched place. If it weren't for his hound running inside the courtyard, he'd gladly turn around and leave right now. "Trapper!" he called out, hearing the dog barking from somewhere inside the castle walls.

"Leave now, before we're forced to make ye go." Another guard from atop the battlements pulled back a bowstring with an arrow aimed right at Ethan.

"What in the Clootie's name are ye doin'?" shouted Ethan in surprise. "Put down the bow! I'm leavin'," he said, lifting his hands in the air. What the hell was the matter with these people? They were the most unfriendly lot of people he'd ever encountered in his life.

Ethan pretended to go but, instead, snuck around the back of the castle where he was sure there must be some sort of hidden postern gate. Now, if only he could find it. The winds picked up, blowing his cloak around him and sending a chill up his spine.

He was getting that bad feeling again. It was like something was about to happen and he shouldn't be here.

The castle was in disrepair, with the outer curtain wall crumbling. He walked over the dry moat and pushed his way through the small opening that led to the wall of the inner bailey. Stopping directly under the window of a tower, he looked up, surveying the situation. There were thick vines on the walls and he was sure he could climb them if he tried. If he could just peek over the battlements, he might be able to spot his hound.

Holding on tightly to the vines, Ethan shimmied up the wall. It was high, but he was an experienced climber and had no trouble. When he got to the top, he hesitantly poked his head over the wall, surprised by what he saw. A little girl with dark curly hair and big brown eyes stared at him, her face bathed in moonlight.

"Hello," he said, wondering what a young girl this age was doing unsupervised atop the battlements at night. He swore she had to be no more than about four years of age. She held a doll clutched to her chest that looked to be made of old rags in colors of red and blue. "Have ye seen a big white dog?" he asked, hoisting one leg up to the top of the battlements. "My hound, Trapper, is lost and I'm tryin' to find him."

The little girl nodded and pointed down into the court-yard. "The doggy is down there." When Ethan got one leg over the wall, he heard barking and caught a glimpse of Trapper in the courtyard with several guards chasing him. That was probably why there were no guards on the battlements to stop him.

"Ah, there he is. Now, I'll just have to find a way to sneak him out. Is there by any chance a hidden postern door nearby?"

The little girl once again nodded and pointed, this time to a wall covered in ivy, right behind the gong pit. "There's one down there."

"It figures," he grumbled, not wanting to have to walk knee-deep through human waste to escape with his dog. "Oh well, if that's what it takes," he said, starting to hoist himself over the wall. He stopped abruptly when he heard the blood-curdling scream of a woman coming from the tower directly above him. His head jerked upward and he saw what looked like the body of a falling woman. A whoosh of air went right past him, as well as a fluttering white gown and long, black hair trailing in the breeze.

"Losh me! What was that?" He was so startled at hearing and seeing the ghost so close up that he lost his grip on the wall. As he fell backward, his eyes fastened to the little girl still watching him curiously. She didn't even seem shaken by what they'd just witnessed.

"Naaaaaay!" he cried out as he fell, trying to grab at the vines along the way so he wouldn't break his damned neck when he hit the ground. He landed with a thud on his back, thankfully falling atop something soft. When he smelled the stench, he realized that he'd fallen into a large mound of horse manure that was hidden under dead leaves and a dusting of snow. Then again, mayhap he was closer to the garderobe than he thought. He could only hope it was a mare's nest that was now smeared over his cloak and plaid and not something else. "God's teeth, this isna turnin' out to be a guid night at all."

From his position on the ground, he could see the tower above him in the moonlight. To his surprise, a very beautiful woman peered out the tower window and glanced down to the ground. Her hair was long and blond and she wore a dark cloak over her plaid. The wind blew her hood from her head. Her eyes met his, and when they did, his mouth fell open. He couldn't move nor could he believe what he saw.

Flat on his back and looking up at the sky, the woman looked very familiar to Ethan. Mayhap he'd died and gone to heaven or perhaps he was transported into the past somehow because he knew that girl! Aye, he recognized her face and it was one he despised as well as never wanted to forget for as long as he lived.

"Alana?" he said in confusion, blinking a few more times, not sure if he was only hallucinating because of the fall he'd just taken. Perhaps he'd hit his head.

The woman raised her hood, covering her head and hiding her face. Then she slowly stepped back into the shadows of the tower.

"Alana!" he called out again. Then he was distracted by an animal licking his face. "There ye are, Trapper." He sat up and checked himself for broken bones. Thankfully, he didn't find any. "Trapper, ye are in big trouble, boy," he scolded the dog, standing up and brushing off his hands and plaid as best as possible. He could have stayed to investigate the ghost, but he didn't want to. He was so shaken right now that all he wanted to do was leave. "Come on, boy. Let's get the hell out of here before we're hit with another ghost."

He made his way down to the water, just as Hawke and Oliver were starting to sail away without him. "Hold up," he called out, running for the boat with Trapper leading the way.

"It's about time ye got here. I wasna goin' to wait," snorted Hawke.

"I can see that," remarked Ethan, getting into the boat. His dog followed.

"Where the hell were ye and what is that wretched smell?"

"Ye wouldna believe me if I told ye," said Ethan, settling himself on the seat. He looked over at Oliver who was sitting there with a frown on his face, sulking. "Did ye find yer sister's doll, lad?"

"Nay," snapped Oliver. "It's gone forever and now Sophie will never stop cryin'."

"Well, then there's no need to ever come back here." Ethan looked back toward the castle high on the cliff. He was still shaken from hearing the scream of the dead woman and seeing her body fall right past him. But what haunted him even more than that was the fact he saw Alana in the tower window, because he never thought he'd ever see his past betrothed again.

CHAPTER 2

"What did ye say?" asked Kirstine, brushing little Isobel's hair as she and Alana got ready for bed in the main solar.

"I said I looked out the tower window after I played the ghost, and I saw Ethan MacKeefe. I'm sure it was him although Diarmad said he was dead." Alana wrung her hands and paced the solar floor. She was overwhelmed with emotions. She had thought her lover was dead but now she wasn't so sure. Hope filled her that it really was Ethan she saw.

"Ye saw Ethan?" gasped Kirstine. "Alana, perhaps it was his ghost."

"Nay, he was just as real as ye and me. Or, at least I think he was."

"Well, if so, what would he be doin' here? No one comes to this isle."

"I'm no' sure. But I'm guessin' that hound that wandered into the courtyard was really his after all. It all makes sense now. He was here lookin' for his dog."

"Did he see ye?" asked her sister anxiously.

Alana bit her lip and shrugged. "I dinna ken for sure. Even if he did, I canna be certain he kent it was me. At least he left before Diarmad saw him."

"Sister, ye have had a hard night and should get some rest. Then mayhap ye'll stop seein' hauntin' visions of the man ye were supposed to marry."

"Haud yer wheesht!" Alana warned her, throwing her a nasty glare. Alana didn't want her daughter hearing too much about Ethan. "Time for bed, sweetie," she said, guiding the little girl to the bed they shared. That is when she noticed her daughter holding a doll she'd never seen before. "Did ye give her that doll?" Alana asked her sister.

"Nay, I thought ye did," replied Kirstine.

"Who's Ethan?" asked Isobel. "Is he that nice man I saw up on the battlements?"

"Isobel, quiet," said Alana, trying to think. "And that reminds me. What were ye doin' up on the battlements? Ye are no' supposed to go up there alone."

"My dolly wanted to go for a walk." The little girl held tightly to the doll that Alana had never seen before.

"Where did ye get that?" asked Alana.

"My friend gave it to me. It was her dolly, but now it's mine." Isobel hugged the doll and kissed it.

"Isobel, stop lyin'," said Alana, tired of the little girl making up stories these past few years. It had really started getting out of control lately. She supposed it was because Isobel was lonely and didn't have any other children to play with. There were no other children in the castle besides Isobel's uncle, Finn. But Finn was much older than Isobel and certainly didn't play with dolls! "Get in bed," she commanded, taking the doll from the girl.

Isobel whined and started to cry, holding out her hands.

"Oh, all right. I guess there is no harm in havin' it. It's only a toy." She gave the doll back, and the child stopped crying. Then she tucked her in and kissed her. Afterwards, she walked into the antechamber to speak to Kirstine where the little girl couldn't overhear them.

"Alana, if ye really did see Ethan MacKeefe tonight, that is no' a guid thing. Especially if he saw ye," explained Kirstine. She rubbed her large belly as she spoke.

"I ken." Alana felt concern welling within her chest. "Kirstine, I hate this life of livin' in secret as naught more than prisoners. And I despise the fact that ye are Diarmad's wife."

"Alana, mayhap it's no' so bad," she answered, faking a smile, looking down at her belly. "At least I will have a child to love even if I hate the child's faither."

"Nay. It's no' right and ye ken it. I wish we could leave here and never see Diarmad again."

"Mayhap we should try to escape," suggested Kirstine, surprising Alana. Every time Alana had brought up the idea, Kirstine was the one to reject it. Of course, Kirstine was always worrying about Alana and Isobel and would do anything to keep them safe. Even be the wife of their captor and not complain.

Alana had been seriously thinking about leaving lately, and taking her family with her. Now that they were back in Scotland, it would be easier she supposed. But Diarmad chained her father to the bed now when he left on smuggling runs since her father was becoming too ill to travel with him. She feared what might happen to the rest of them if her father died. This was Diarmad's way of controlling Alana and her siblings because he knew she would never leave her father behind. But with Kirstine being the man's wife and ready to birth him another baby, it only complicated matters.

"Finn is almost done workin' on buildin' the boat," whispered Alana. It was a secret project using the wood from the abandoned hut where Osla and her children used to live. "Mayhap when the time is right, we can try it out."

"Diarmad will be leavin' soon on another run," said Kirstine. "Mayhap Albert and Graeme will help us."

"I want to leave, Kirstine, I really do," said Alana with a sigh. "But we have nowhere to go even if we do get off this isle. Faither has seen to it that no one will ever welcome us back again. And if we show up in public, we are most likely goin' to be thrown in the dungeon for Faither's crimes. If they tie us to the smugglin' ring, we might all hang for it."

"I see yer point, Alana. Ye are right. I guess we have no choice but to stay here. After all, I am Diarmad's wife now and soon to have his baby. Mayhap ye and Finn should go without me."

"I would never do that and ye ken it. Damn, why did Faither ever get hooked up with the vile man to begin with?"

"Dinna be angry with Faither," said Kirstine. "He loves us, but just has a problem of makin' the wrong choices too often."

"I ken," she agreed. "And since Mathair's death, he has seemed to lose the will to live. With Mathair's dyin' breath, she told me to forgive him, and so I will."

"She also told ye to guard the treasure, but we've yet to even find it."

"I have a suspicion that we are closer than ye think," said Alana, pulling the key out from around her neck attached to a string. It was hidden under her shirt. Her wedding ring was on the string with the key. "I think the treasure might be hidden right here at Blackbriar."

"Really?" Kirstine's eyes opened wide. "It would be a guid place to hide it since everyone is afraid to step foot on the isle."

"My thoughts exactly. Our uncle kent this and so did our mathair."

"Doesna Faither ken where the treasure is hidden?"

"Nay. I'm sure he wasna told because with his little problem, he couldna be trusted."

"I wonder why our family was chosen to guard it?" asked Kirstine. "I would like to ken more."

"Me, too, but I dinna think we'll ever find out. But I'm goin' to find the treasure if it's the last thing I ever do. And then, I'm goin' to use it."

"Use it? For what?"

"To start a new life far away from here where no one even kens who we are. I dinna want my daughter livin' like this. It is no' right. And ye should no' have to be married to a man ye dinna love."

"Then we are goin' to escape after all? I'm confused." Kirstine held on to the wall for balance. "And are we goin' to bring Faither with us?"

"Shhhh," said Alana, her eyes darting around. "One of Diarmad's men might hear ye talkin'."

"Alana, mayhap it's time we get help. If Ethan is truly still alive, then mayhap he and the MacKeefes can –"

"Nay! Now haud yer wheesht," spat Alana. "I could never ask Ethan and his friends to risk their lives to help me after the pain I've inflicted on them. Especially, after leavin' Ethan at the altar on our weddin' day."

"Mayhap he still has eyes for ye, Alana. Perhaps all isna really lost after all."

"It's over, Kirstine," Alana said softly, wishing things could be different. "What Ethan and I had could have been beautiful but I made the decision to leave him. No man will ever forgive an action like that. Besides, I'm sure he thinks I am naught but a traitor."

"Mayhap no'. After all, ye thought he was dead and now ye found out he isna. Talk to Faither. Tell him Ethan was on the isle and is still alive. After all, the MacKeefe camp is close by. Mayhap more of them will come here. Mayhap Faither will come up with a plan."

"Nay, no one else will come here. We've seen to that, or have ye forgotten? Our deceit will be kept a secret because of the awful legend that we canna let die. Kirstine, I didna want to alarm ye, but Faither's health has been gettin' worse lately. Bein' chained up is killin' his spirit and makin' things even worse. He is too weak to go on the smugglin' runs, yet Diarmad willna let him be. He is close to death, I am sure of it. It is even hard to carry on a conversation with him anymore."

"What will happen to us if he dies before Diarmad says his debt is paid off?"

"I'm afraid if that happens, we will be stranded here for the rest of our lives. The secret boat Finn is makin' is almost finished. So when it is, I will take it for a test before we all use it to sail to the mainland if we do decide to escape."

"Alana, we are trapped in a life of hell that we will never escape, isna that so?" She sadly looked down at the bump that proved she would never be free of the evil man who forced her to be his bride.

"Nay," Alana told her, putting her arm around her sister's shoulders. Trying to remain optimistic was getting harder and harder through the years. "We'll find a way out of this, dinna ye worry."

"But it has been so long. I miss Mathair more and more each day."

"Me, too," said Alana, rubbing her sister's shoulder.

"Do ye ever miss Ethan?" asked Kirstine.

"More than ye ken," she replied. "Because of my decision, I have given up the only man I have ever loved. I had given up all hope of ever bein' happy. But after seein' Ethan today, and findin' out he is still alive, it makes me start to wonder about a lot of things."

"What do ye mean?"

"I mean, I wonder if Ethan and I could have been happy together."

"I'm sure ye would have been."

"Kirstine," said Alana, grabbing her sister's arm. "Do ye think . . . do ye think Ethan is married and perhaps has a bunch of children by now?"

Kirstine made a face and shrugged. "Alana, it has been five years. I dinna think the man would have waited that long and no' have gotten married. After all, he is a Highland warrior. He is one of the mighty MacKeefes. I'm sorry to say it, but he has probably found someone else by now."

"I ken ye are right," said Alana, looking across the room at her daughter, sleeping soundly in the large bed. The little girl hugged her mysterious doll. "I – I just wish I could have told Ethan about Isobel. But now . . . now I'll never be able to tell him. Even if I happen to see him again, it is too late. If he is married and has bairns, I will take my secret to my grave rather than disrupt his life again. Nay, what Ethan and I had is over. And even if I see him again someday, I can never tell him that he has a daughter."

CHAPTER 3

"*E*than ye look like death warmed over." Ethan's friends, Logan and Caleb, came to join Hawke and Ethan at the fire of the MacKeefe camp the next morning. Each of the men was the son of one of the well-known MacKeefes. While Hawke was the son of the clan's laird, Storm MacKeefe, the rest of the three friends were sons of the Madmen MacKeefe. Logan was the son of Aidan. Caleb's father was Ian, and Ethan was the son of Onyx.

Since it was nearly winter, most of the MacKeefes were in residence at Hermitage Castle on the border right now. The MacKeefes claimed the castle in a battle against the English and had controlled it for years now. But some of the MacKeefes chose to stay in the Highlands, even though the upcoming winter would most likely be a hard one.

The hills of the MacKeefe lands were spotted with long-haired cattle and black-faced sheep that were able to stay warm in the winter cold. They were used for milk and to feed the clan. Ethan and his friends normally stayed here most of the year to tend to them so they'd have food for their clan through the winter.

"Nay, no' death," said Hawke, lifting a tankard of Mountain Magic to his mouth. Mountain Magic was the strongest whisky in all of Scotland, brewed by Hawke's great-grandfather, Old Callum MacKeefe, who was older than the hills. He swore the Mountain Magic was what kept him alive so long. "Ethan claims to have seen another ghost last night." Hawke's red tail hawk, Apollo, screeched from up in the sky. He looked up at it, using his hand to block the sun from his eyes. "Or at least, that's what he says."

"A ghost? Did I hear ye say somethin' about a ghost?" A young woman named Bridget stood nearby talking with her father, Brigham. She craned her neck and looked over toward the fire. Her father was the chronicler of the Scottish king.

"Bid the devil," mumbled Ethan to his friends, running a hand over the head of his wolfhound that lay at his feet. "I dinna want those two anywhere near me."

"Why no'?" asked Caleb. "Bridget and her faither are very nice." Caleb looked up and smiled as the girl and her father started toward them. His eyes lit up and he looked like a lovesick boy. Caleb was the smallest of Ethan's friends, but also the fastest. His curly dark hair hung down to his shoulders, reminding Ethan of one of the wooly Highland sheep.

"They watch everythin' we do and listen to everythin' we say," complained Logan in a low voice, not being fond of the visitors either. "I dinna ken why they followed us here to the Highlands. I wish they would have stayed back at Hermitage Castle instead." Logan looked a lot like his father, Aidan, being the only blond out of their group of friends. His pet of choice was a wolf named Jack that usually stayed away from everyone, hiding in the shadows. His wolf accompanied him wherever he went and was an asset when it came to hunting during their travels.

"Dinna ye want to be mentioned in the king's book – the Highland Chronicles?" asked Caleb. "After all, Hawke is mentioned in the book now, as well as all of our faithers."

"Sure I do," complained Ethan, spearing a piece of meat on a stick and holding it over the open fire to cook. "Who wouldna want to be? It's one of the highest honors."

He pulled his cloak closer around him. The breeze was becoming colder each day, and with it would come the winds of change. "I just dinna want to be mentioned in the book as the man who fears ghosts, that's all," he continued.

"Well, it's better than no' bein' mentioned at all." Logan sat down on a rock next to Ethan. He stabbed a piece of meat with a sharp stick and held it over the fire to cook. Caleb sat down next to him. "I dinna think I'll ever get my name in that book."

"Ye two should have seen Ethan last night," said Hawke with a chuckle. "I never saw him look so pale as when he thought I was about to leave him on the isle . . . with the ghost."

"Did somethin' happen last night?" asked Bridget, overhearing the end of their conversation as she approached the group of men. "Please, tell us all about it." She looked around for a place to sit. Caleb immediately jumped up and surrendered his seat to the girl. He stood right behind her, smiling all the while.

"Aye, do tell us," said Brigham, holding on to the Highland Chronicle book that he used to record the deeds of the MacKeefes that were worth mentioning to the king.

"Nothin' happened," mumbled Ethan, pulling the meat out of the fire and inspecting it. "I lost my hound and then I found it. That's all." He blew on the meat and, with two fingers, pulled it off the stick. It was hot so he dropped it atop his lap on his plaid to cool. Trapper whined, eyeing the food. "It's no' yers, boy," he told the dog. "I'll get ye somethin' to eat when I'm finished. But right now, I'm famished."

"We went to the isle with Oliver, looking for his sister's doll," explained Hawke, biting into an apple. "And then Ethan disappeared and came back covered in horse dung."

Ethan's friends all laughed.

"And I was blamin' the stench on his dog," said Logan, reaching out to pet the wolfhound on the head. "I'm sorry, Trapper."

"Och, I am no longer wearin' the soiled plaid, and I washed in the loch last night and froze my arse doin' it," said Ethan in his defense. "So if I hear another word about it, the one who says somethin' will be the next to go for a little swim – courtesy of me."

Suddenly everyone was quiet and busied themselves looking away from Ethan.

With his head still down, Ethan glanced up at Hawke and scowled. He wanted to muffle him right now, because he knew where this conversation was leading and he didn't like it.

"I am guessin' by the way the lass was cryin' all night that ye didna find the doll," said Brigham, walking around the fire and sitting down on a stump used as a stool.

"Nay, we didna," said Hawke. "Of course, Oliver and I could have used a little more help." He glared back at Ethan when he said it.

"I'm confused," said Bridget, looking at Hawke and then over to Ethan. "Werena ye with them, Ethan? And how did ye get covered with horse manure?"

"Aye, I was there." Ethan answered without making eye contact with the girl. Instead, he looked down at the food on his lap. Another minute and it would be cool enough to eat. He was already salivating, just thinking of the rich beef. "I was momentarily distracted when my hound took off chasin' someone," Ethan explained. "Of course, I had to follow Trapper to the castle to bring him back."

"The castle?" asked Brigham with interest. "Do ye mean the one that is said to be haunted?"

"That's right! Blackbriar Castle," said Bridget with a nod. "We've heard in our travels that a ghost inhabits it. Supposedly, a woman was murdered there years ago and she can still be heard screamin' as she is pushed from the tower over and over again."

"Heard . . . or seen," mumbled Ethan into his cup as he took a swig of Mountain Magic.

"Seen?" Bridget's blue eyes grew wide and she leaned forward so as not to miss a single word. "Did ye really see the ghost of Blackbriar Castle while ye were there? How excitin'. Please tell us all about it."

"He no' only saw a ghost, but he thinks he saw Alana, too," Hawke told them.

"Alana?" The chronicler looked up, confused.

"Faither, Alana was his betrothed who left him on their weddin' day," explained Bridget softly.

"She no' only left him, but she made a fool out of him," Caleb joined in.

"That's right," added Logan. "She never planned on

marryin' Ethan at all. It was only a ploy – a distraction. She worked with her thievin' faither. While we were distracted with the preparations for the weddin', they stole our livestock and tried to sell it to the MacDougals."

"Really?" said Bridget looking over at her father. She took the Highland Chronicles from him and put the book on her lap. "So Ethan's bride was really naught but a bandit?"

"Nay!" shouted Ethan, not wanting anyone to talk of this hurtful incident again. Part of him wanted to badmouth his past betrothed for what she did. It angered him and hurt him deeply. But somewhere in his heart, Ethan was still in love with Alana, and might always be. After seeing her at the castle, he tossed and turned all night going over scenarios in his head, wondering which of them was true. He was so confused and upset that just the mention of Alana's name made him crazy.

Ethan grimaced and ran a hand through his hair, cursing himself inwardly for ever going to the island in the first place. He didn't know how to answer Bridget because he didn't want any of this getting into the Highland Chronicles. Then again, it didn't matter, because before he could say another word, Caleb's pesky pine marten jumped atop Ethan's lap. It stole the piece of meat, and slinked away into the shadows before he knew what happened.

"Och, nay!" shouted Ethan, jumping to his feet. "Get back here ye doitit bandit!" Just that word, bandit, made his heart ache again, thinking of what Bridget had just called the woman he once loved and wanted to spend the rest of his life with. But that was a long time ago, and his relationship with Alana was over.

Trapper jumped up, his eyes interlocking with Ethan's,

waiting for his command. "All right. Go get him, boy," said Ethan, giving his dog permission to hunt down the little thief. The hound took off at a run, chasing the little weasel through the camp, knocking things over along the way.

"Nay! Stop yer hound, Ethan," shouted Caleb. "He's goin' to kill Slink."

"Slink?" asked Ethan. "I thought yer pine marten's name was Marty."

"Well, it was, but I changed it to Slink. I like that better." Caleb took off at a run after his pet.

"If ye'll excuse me," said Ethan, nodding to the chronicler and his daughter and chasing after his hound. Honestly, he was glad to get away from them. But now he had to stop his dog before it devoured Caleb's stupid pet. As far as he was concerned, a pine marten was no good and no better than a skunk or a weasel. It certainly was not a good choice for a pet at all. What had Caleb been thinking? Caleb sometimes made addlepated decisions, and this one had to top them all.

"I've got him," called out Oliver, hunkering down, and calling the dog to him. The wolfhound liked the boy and ran to him, lying down at his feet. Oliver held on to the dog's neck while Caleb continued to chase Slink. Since his pet was new, Caleb did not yet have the skill of making it listen to him. Then again, Ethan's dog had a mind of his own as well.

"Thank ye, Oliver," said Ethan, crouching down next to the boy to pet the wolfhound. "I'm sorry that we werena able to find yer sister's doll."

"I want my dolly," cried the boy's sister, Sophie, running to them and hugging her brother. Ethan's heart went out to the little girl. She seemed so sad.

"It must be a special doll," Ethan told her. "Did your mathair make it for ye?"

"Aye, she did," the girl answered, wiping a tear from her eye with the back of her hand. "My mathair made it out of her own clothes. But now Isobel has it."

"Why does Isobel have it?" asked Ethan, trying to calm the girl down by talking with her.

"I gave it to her, but I want it back."

"Well, mayhap we can find ye another doll," Ethan suggested, managing to get a big pout from her in return. "What did it look like?"

"Her doll was made of rags and was wearin' a blue and red dress," said her brother. "But she has no friend named Isobel. We were the only children on the isle. Sophie made that part up."

"I dinna!" screamed the girl, looking furious with her brother for saying that. Oliver gave her a look that said he wanted the girl to stay quiet about something.

"I see." Suddenly, a vision flashed through Ethan's mind of the little girl he saw yesterday at the castle. "Sophie, ye said ye had a friend named Isobel?"

"Aye," she said, wiping her eyes. "I did. Honest, I did."

"Nay, she's lyin'," said Oliver, making Sophie start to cry again.

"Was the little girl, perhaps livin' at the castle?" asked Ethan.

"Aye," said Sophie. "But she sneaked out to play with me sometimes."

"Sophie, hush," said Oliver in a warning tone. "Mathair wouldna like it if she kent ye were makin' up stories again."

Just the mention of their dead mother upset the girl and she started bawling once again.

"Now wait a moment." Ethan held up a hand to the girl's brother. "I do believe ye, Sophie."

"Ye do?" She looked up and blinked her wet lashes twice.

"Aye, because I think I saw yer friend, Isobel yesterday," Ethan explained. "At the castle."

"Ye did?" Hope showed in Sophie's eyes.

"Aye, and she was holdin' a doll that sounds very similar to the one ye described."

"I want to play with Isobel," said Sophie. "I want my dolly back."

"That's goin' to be a little hard to do since the castle is haunted," continued Ethan. "I, for one, dinna ever plan on goin' back there again."

Sophie released her brother and ran to Ethan, wrapping her arms around him. She sobbed and looked up to him with those sad eyes. Tears rolled down her cheeks. "Please, find my dolly for me. Please, Ethan."

Ethan picked up the little girl and stood up, holding her to his chest in a protective hug. She was cold and her little body shook like a leaf. This doll meant the world to her. She needed it to comfort her now that her mother had died. How could he tell her that he wouldn't help her? He would seem like naught but an ogre if he turned her away.

"Och, lass," he said, rubbing her back and looking out over the water in the distance toward the isle. He kept thinking of seeing Alana in the tower and part of him longed to go back to find out if it was true. "Mayhap I can try to find yer doll for ye, but I canna promise ye that I will."

"Oh, thank ye," said the little girl, kissing him on the cheek and looking up at him like he was some sort of savior. Ethan wasn't a savoir, and the last thing he wanted was to step foot on that blasted isle again. But how could he turn down the request of a poor child who had naught left in life but her brother? Everyone needed a comfort item to make them feel safe, and hers was her doll. It was the last remembrance of her departed mother. Knowing this, nothing else seemed to matter. He had to find that doll for her because he wanted to make the little girl smile.

"Oh, it's no' a problem," said Ethan, already feeling a knot twisting in his gut. He always thought Caleb was the one who made addlepated decisions. But now, he was the one doing just that. After all, he'd just agreed to purposely go back to Blackbriar Castle.

CHAPTER 4

*T*he sky darkened overhead as Ethan stepped into the boat later that day, preparing to go back to the cursed isle. Part of him wanted naught to do with the wretched place, but he was going for more reasons than one. The first one being to help the little girl so she'd stop crying. The second, because he needed to find out if it truly was Alana he saw in the tower window.

"We'd better hurry," said Hawke, untying the boat as Trapper jumped in over the side. "It looks like there is one hell of a storm brewin'."

Hawke insisted on going with Ethan to the isle since Sophie was now in his care. Even if the girl wasn't his by birth, he had an instant family with Oliver and Sophie, being married to Phoebe.

"Mayhap we'd better wait until the storm passes," said Ethan, glancing up at the sky. Yesterday was nothing with the light wind and flurry of snow. Today looked like the sky was about to open and a blizzard was going to cover the land.

"Nay, my ears canna take the wee lass' cryin' a minute

longer," grumbled Hawke. "If ye say ye ken where this doll is, then God's eyes, get it fast!"

Just as Hawke was about to push off, Caleb came running down the hill to the loch. "Wait!" he called, waving his arms as the wind picked up and the snow started to fall.

"What is it?" asked Hawke. "Is somethin' wrong?"

"Aye," said Caleb. "Oliver decided he was goin' to tend to the cows and sheep."

"And what's wrong with that?" asked Hawke. "He's done it before when he lived on the isle. He kens how to do it."

"Mayhap, but the boy is careless. He let half the herd wander off. We need ye back at camp, Hawke. Since most of the men are back at Hermitage Castle, we need ye both to help get the herd into the barn before the storm sets in. It looks like it's goin' to be a bad one."

Normally, the livestock stayed outside all year long in the hills surrounding the MacKeefe camp. But when it looked like they'd have a lot of snow, they moved them inside so it made it easier to manage when they had to supplement their feedings. This way they wouldn't have to move them through the snow.

"All right," said Hawke with a sigh. "I'm comin'."

"Trapper will help round up the sheep as well as any cattle that might have gone astray." Ethan stood up, half-relieved to be staying instead of going to the isle after all.

"Nay." Hawke held up a hand. "We dinna need ye. Ye go to the isle, get the doll, and get back before the water is too choppy to sail."

"But . . . but Trapper can round up the herd faster than us. And I need to be here to give him commands."

"Logan's wolf, Jack, can do the same thing," stated Hawke.

"Now sit back down and get over to the isle and find that doitit doll before my head splits open with the lassie's cryin'."

"Pay my respects to the ghost," said Caleb as he started laughing and walking away.

Ethan looked out over the water that was already getting choppy. The wind picked up and was blowing the snow at an angle now. He could hardly even see across to the isle. "It looks like it'll take two of us to sail the boat in this weather."

"Ye're right," said Hawke. "Caleb, go with him."

"What? Me?" Caleb suddenly stopped in his tracks and turned around. His laughing ceased and his mouth turned down into a frown. "Nay, ye go, Hawke."

"What's the matter, Caleb? Is there a reason ye dinna want to go?" Ethan asked him.

"Well . . . nay, of course no'. I dinna believe in ghosts if that is what ye're thinkin'." Caleb looked down and brushed off his plaid as he spoke. "I just canna go because I need to find Slink before the storm sets in."

"Ye're in luck, because he's right there." Hawke pointed down at the ground. The pine marten ran up to Caleb, getting on its back legs, trying to reach up to him. Caleb scooped up the animal and cradled it in his arms. "Fine, I'll go," he spat. "But if we lose any of the herd because I wasna here to help ye, then ye are goin' to have to explain it to our laird."

"Dinna worry, we willna lose a single one as long as I'm here," Hawke assured him. "Besides, Apollo will help by spottin' them from the air. Now, go! And dinna return without that doll or I'll wring both yer necks!"

"Dinna fash yerself, I'll get the blasted doll," grumbled Ethan. "And I promise ye, this is the last time I will ever set foot on the isle or inside that castle, so dinna ask again."

* * *

"Faither, please. Ye need to drink if ye are goin' to get better." Alana helped her father to a sitting position in bed, holding the cup to his mouth to give him some water.

"Dinna waste yer time with me, Alana," said Gil, after taking a sip. "My health is failin' quickly. I willna live through the winter, and we both ken it."

"Nay! Dinna say that." She put the cup down, fluffed his feather pillow and tried to help him get comfortable. Diarmad and his men had left him behind again, sailing out with the smuggled goods to meet their contact, leaving him chained to the bed. It was a horrible thing to do and it disgusted Alana. After all this time and Diarmad still didn't trust her father.

"Alana, take yer sister and brathair and leave this isle. I'm sure Albert and Graeme will help ye make it to the mainland safely if I ask them to."

"Nay. Ye ken we willna leave without ye."

"I'm too weak to travel. Besides, now that I'm chained to the bed I'll be goin' nowhere. Now find them and go. This is no life for any of ye. Especially my granddaughter and grand-child to be. Plus, Kirstine needs a chance to find a man she can love and trust. So do ye."

"I've never heard ye talk that way before," said Alana, perusing her father. "It almost sounds as if ye dinna agree that gettin' married is only for makin' alliances."

"Yer mathair and I wed for alliances, and I canna say she ever really loved me," he explained. "Then again, I never gave her reason to love me, either. But I fell in love with her the first time I met her."

"I loved Ethan all my life, Da. Yet, ye never seemed to like the idea of me marryin' him."

"Once again, I've made a wrong choice," he told her. "If we could do it all over, I'd support yer marriage to him and I would make an alliance with the MacKeefes instead of makin' them my enemies." He hung his head. "But it's too late to change the past."

"I wish we could change the past," she told him. "Then mathair would still be alive and I'd be married to Ethan."

"I'm sorry about Ethan's death, Daughter. Honest, I am. I had nothin' to do with it. Ye have to believe me. I didna even ken."

"I believe ye, Faither. But Ethan is no' dead. I saw Ethan MacKeefe last night, right here on this isle and at the castle."

"Ye did?" Her father looked confused. "But I thought Diarmad said he was dead."

"That's what he wanted us to think," she explained. "And like fools, we believed it, givin' him more power to control us all."

"Oh, Alana, I am so sorry."

Alana went back to the bedstand, cradling the cup. She seriously started to consider the suggestion of leaving without her father. But then she shook her head and turned to face him. "Nay, Faither, we willna leave without ye. We are in this together to the end. That is what family is for."

"Ye dinna deserve this kind of life, Alana. I've ruined all yer lives and killed yer mathair. I dinna deserve to live."

"Stop that kind of talk." She hurried over to the bed and sat on the edge, taking her father's hands in hers. He looked so frail and gaunt. Ever since her mother died, he had lost his will to live. "Mathair's last words were to forgive ye, and so I have. I understand ye've made some poor decisions in life. We all have. But we canna live our lives in regret. It'll get better soon. I ken it will."

"How can ye say that, Daughter? It's been five years that we've been prisoners of Diarmad. He's forced us to help him smuggle and he's taken yer sister for his wife against her will. We are trapped and doomed to live this life forever."

"Nay, we're no', Faither. We'll find a way to leave now that we're back in Scotland. But we'll do it together."

"None of us are welcome here anymore. Because of me, ye will all be rejected. And when it is discovered that we all had a hand in this deceitful ring of smugglin', we'll be killed or imprisoned for the rest of our lives."

That was the thought that had been running through Alana's mind for quite a while now. They were in too deep to ever get out.

"Mayhap Ethan can help us," she blurted out, testing her father's reaction.

"Nay!" her father bellowed, taking all his energy to do it. "The MacKeefes are our enemies now, just like the MacDougals, the Chisholms and many others. Ye canna ever tell him about this. If so, he'll be sure to tell the others and that will be yer downfall. Ye must keep quiet about all this and tell no one. Do ye understand?"

"But Da! We are talkin' about Ethan. He is the faither of my baby. Certainly he willna do anythin' to risk our lives once he kens he has a child."

"Nay, Alana. Ye must never tell him he's the faither of yer child either," her father said in a strong voice. "He'll take Isobel away from ye, and ye'll hang by the neck or spend the rest of yer life behind bars."

"Nay, Ethan is no' like that. He would never do anythin' to hurt me. I was supposed to be his bride."

"Exactly," said her father, sadness filling his eyes now. "No man will accept that kind of treatment from a lassie. He will hate ye forever for leavin' him at the altar."

"Nay!" Alana dropped her father's hands and sprang to her feet. "He must ken that it wasna my idea to leave him. It was yers, Faither, if ye havena forgotten."

"Aye, it was my idea. And that is why ye and yer siblin's must leave me and go far away. Try to make it to France where no one kens ye."

"France? We dinna have any relations in France and neither do I want to go."

"Ye'll need money," he said, his eyes closing partially. "God kens I've tried to work with Diarmad to pay back my debts and provide a guid life for ye, Kirstine and Finn. And even little Isobel. But I failed, Daughter. So now it is up to ye."

"What do ye mean?"

"I saw yer mathair give ye somethin' before she died even though ye deny it. And I'm sure it has somethin' to do with the hidden treasure."

"I – I dinna ken what ye're talkin' about." She had never told her father. Her hand subconsciously caressed the key hanging from a string around her neck, under her clothes.

"Dinna lie, Alana. It doesna become ye. And I dinna have enough strength left to look for the treasure myself. I ken it is here in the castle, just as ye do."

"What makes ye think that?"

"It only makes sense," he told her. "I was a fool no' to think of it before. One day, yer uncle told me that when he was a boy he used to come to Blackbriar Castle often in secret."

"Uncle Freddie came here? Why?" she asked, not knowing why anyone would do that on purpose. The place was eerie and she didn't even like being here although it was now her home. Still, hearing this confirmed her suspicions.

"I believe he befriended the madman, Murdock who used to live here. I saw them together once or twice. That got me thinkin' lately, that he might have had Murdock hide the treasure. Ye've go to find it, Alana. With it, ye and the others will be able to start a new life far from Scotland."

"Da, I ken very little about this treasure. What can ye tell me?"

He let out a sigh, his eyes still closed and his head back on the pillow as he spoke. "When yer mathair and I were first married, she and her brathair, Freddie, confided in me about the treasure. But through the years when my – bad choices came more and more often, they kept things from me."

"Why do they have this treasure? And it has somethin' to do with the Knights Templar? How can that be? That was so long ago."

"I dinna understand it all, but from what I ken, there was a relative of yer mathair's down the line that once had somethin' to do with the Knights Templar."

"Really," she said, felling a shiver course through her body. "How excitin'. Tell me more."

"As ye ken, most of the Templars were killed off and their treasure went missin'."

"And ye think that we have that treasure?"

"Nay, lass. No' all of it. It was split up and there was a lot of it." He let out another sigh. "Supposedly, yer mathair's family was entrusted with a small part of it. It was left with them and they were to guard it until . . . until some other guardian of the Knights Templar came to pick it up."

"For this many years?" she asked. "And ye think they havena got it yet? So what happened to this person who was the courier?"

"I dinna ken, lass. Like I said, yer mathair and uncle stopped confidin' in me. All I ken was that this treasure was supposed to be protected and kept out of the wrong hands. Like mine, I suppose."

Alana had been thinking the same thing, but didn't want to say it. Even with all her father's vices and all the wrong he had done, he was still her father. She loved him and forgave him. Alana had hope that somehow, some way, she could help him redeem himself. However, after this much time had passed, her fate had been slipping away rapidly.

"Mathair gave me a key," she told him, pulling it out from under her clothes and holding it up for him to see. Her wedding ring dangled on the string with it. "But I dinna ken what it opens, or where the treasure might be."

"A key?" He pushed up to a sitting position, narrowing his eyes to see it. "That's the key to our answers," he said, getting that look in his eyes he always got when he was about to do something stupid, thinking he was going to get rich fast.

"Alana," she heard her sister calling from somewhere in the castle.

"Dinna let Diarmad ken ye have that," he told her in a low voice. "He would kill to get that treasure. Let me see it, lass." He held out his hand.

Suddenly, she regretted showing it to him. She hated this feeling because she wanted more than anything to trust her father, but a little part of her still told her to beware. Her father wasn't known for keeping secrets, or for being moral in any way. As much as she loved him, maybe it truly was too late to redeem him. And now it was too late to keep things from him because he'd seen the key.

This made her sad, but she had her siblings and her daughter to think about now. She had to be careful, even around her father.

"I willna let Diarmad see it," she said, shoving it back under her clothes. "I must go now, Faither. Kirstine calls for me, and ye need to rest."

She turned and headed for the door.

"Alana," he said, causing her to stop and look back over her shoulder. "I ken ye dinna trust me, and Lord kens I've never given ye a reason to. But I need ye to believe me now when I say I would give my life to free ye and yer siblin's."

"I ken that, Da," she said softly, feeling a tear forming in her eye.

"I would do anythin' to have yer mathair back, but it is too late for that. But it is no' too late for me to help ye find the treasure to ensure ye have a guid life after all. I dinna want it for myself or to trade away. I want it . . . I want to find it . . . so ye can someday be free. So ye can marry a man ye love . . . and be happy the way ye used to be."

Alana bit her lip to keep from crying. Her father was right. At one time she was very happy, when she was going to be married to Ethan. But she gave all that up to help her family, even though she, and they, became prisoners in the end.

"Get some rest, Da," she told him, having a lot to think about. "Ye arena responsible for my happiness, or for what happens to me, Kirstine, Finn or even Isobel."

"But . . . I am yer faither," he said. "I need to take care of ye all." He stopped talking and sank down into the pillow, looking so defeated and small. "It seems I have ruined no' only my own life, but I have put the nail in the coffin for the rest of ye as well. Let me redeem myself before I leave this world, Daughter. Give me at least that, if ye will."

"We'll talk later, Da," she told him. "Right now, there is a storm comin' and I need to see that things are taken care of since Diarmad and his men have still no' returned."

"Devil take them in the storm," spat her father through gritted teeth. "I was a fool for too long, and I willna play the victim anymore."

"Da? What are ye sayin'?" she asked, hoping her father wasn't going to try anything stupid. "Dinna anger Diarmad. I will find a way out of here for all of us, and a way to clear our names as well."

"If ye can do that, Daughter, then ye are a godsend. Because without that treasure, ye can consider all of us dead."

His words shook her nerves badly, and Alana turned and ran from the room. With the way her father was talking, she had a bad feeling he was going to try to do something to help and instead get them all killed. She had to come up with an answer quickly, before their lives were doomed forever, just like he said.

"Alana, there ye are," said Kirstine, hurrying across the courtyard as fast as she could in her pregnant state as Alana exited the castle. "The storm is gettin' worse," she told her, pulling the hood of her cloak up over her head.

"Aye," answered Alana. "Did Finn manage to get all the sheep into the barn?" Even though the sheep were smuggled and Alana hated that fact, some of them were kept on the isle for them to consume. Without them, they would starve. She had to be a part of this deceit because their lives depended on it.

"Nay. He's no' back yet and I'm worried," answered her sister. "That's why I called for ye. Ever since Osla and her children left the isle, Finn has been tendin' the sheep, but it is too much for one boy to do alone."

"I agree," said Alana.

"I'm goin' to go out there and help him." Kirstine started for the stable to get her horse.

"Nay," answered Alana, running after her. Kirstine wasn't the best rider to begin with, and Alana didn't want her on a horse this far along in her pregnancy. For her to go out in a storm would only give Alana one more thing to worry about. "I'll go. Ye stay here with Isobel and Faither. Take Isobel to Faither's bedside with ye and make certain she doesna disappear again, like she has a habit of doin' lately."

"Are ye sure?" asked Kirstine, almost being pushed over by a big puff of wind.

"We both ken ye are in no condition to be on a horse let alone out in a storm. I am twice as guid of a rider than ye anyway. Plus, I dinna think ye can get a sheep to listen to ye if yer life depended on it."

"I ken ye're right," answered Kirstine with a giggle. It was so good to see her smile again. It reminded Alana of their days growing up in the clan. Kirstine was such a happy child. But now, she never had cause to smile anymore. "I'm better suited for sewin' and skills inside the keep. Or possibly tendin' to the sick, like Faither."

Alana had never been one to be content with doing the chores of a lady. Neither did she have the patience or skills to be a healer. She liked the rugged Highlands and always felt comfortable in the wilderness and around animals of all kinds.

"I'll help Finn secure the flock and be back in no time at all. Now go and watch over Isobel and Faither please. We'll have to ride out the storm alone since I'm sure Diarmad and his men willna be able to sail back in this weather."

"Guid," said her sister, with hatred showing in her eyes. "I hope Diarmad and the others are swept out to sea and never return!"

Alana felt the same way, but she had to be strong for her sister. "Dinna say that, Kirstine. For the bairn's sake. After all, no matter how much we hate the man, he is still the faither of yer unborn child."

Kirstine rubbed her belly, bit her bottom lip to keep from crying, and nodded slowly. "Ye are right, Sister. I will be strong. For my bairn."

"We'll get through this, Kirstine. I promise ye that we will. I will find a way for our lives to be guid again. But for now, we just need to concern ourselves with gettin' through the storm."

"All right. Be careful," Kirstine called out from behind her as Alana made her way to the stable and collected her horse. She didn't want to waste time with a saddle, so she rode the horse bareback across the drawbridge and up the cliff to where the sheep often grazed.

By the time she got to the field, the snow was mixed with slushy rain and was coming down twice as hard. She could barely see the hand in front of her face.

"Finn! Finn, are ye out here?" she called out, seeing a shadow ahead of her.

"Alana, I canna get the last three sheep into the stable,"

Finn called out through the storm. The boy battled the wind, climbing higher on the steep rocks. It was too dangerous and Alana became frightened for him. "They went higher instead and now they're stuck there."

"God's eyes," she said, directing her horse up the cliff, not really sure how to get the sheep secure so they wouldn't get injured or sick in the storm. "Go back to the barn, Finn. I'll get them. Be ready to open the gate," she told the boy.

"Aye," said Finn, running through the snow. He was on foot and she figured his horse was tied up inside the shelter.

As Alana got closer to the sheep, her horse started to slip. She began to slip as well and regretted not saddling the horse after all. She figured if she could get high enough, she'd come up behind the sheep and scare them down the cliff and right into the pen. Easier said than done. The storm was nasty and it fought against her. Before she knew what happened, her horse slipped and she slid, falling to the ground and hitting her head on the hard, frozen ground.

Her vision blurred – or was it just that it was too hard to see through the snow? She was no longer sure. Her head ached and she thought she heard the barking of a dog in the distance, even though there were no dogs on the isle. Then, just before her eyes closed and she fell into an unconscious state, she swore she saw Ethan MacKeefe's face as he leaned over her body.

* * *

"God's toes, it really is Alana," said Ethan, leaning over the girl he'd seen fall from the horse.

"What's happenin'?" shouted Caleb, climbing the rocks behind him.

"Leave my sister alone," came the shout of a boy from behind them.

Ethan spun around, by nature drawing his sword.

"Dinna hurt me!" The boy held his hands high over his head in surrender and took a step backward. "Ethan?" he asked, looking at him closer. "Is that ye?"

Suddenly, Ethan realized the boy had called Alana his sister. He remembered Alana's siblings, Kirstine and Finn. But when he knew them, Finn was just a child.

"Finn?" he asked. "Ye are so . . . big."

"Aye, it's me," he answered. "I'm three and ten years of age now."

"What are ye doin' out here in the storm?"

"I only want to get the sheep into the pen. I dinna have a weapon, Ethan. Please, dinna hurt me."

Suddenly realizing he was still holding on to his sword, Ethan sheathed his sword to put the boy at ease.

"The sheep?" he asked, not even knowing there were any here. "How many are out in the storm?" He turned and glanced up the hill.

"There are three left. Alana came to help me." The boy looked down to the ground. "Alana? Are ye all right?" Rushing forward, the boy threw himself to his knees at her side.

"Trapper, get the sheep to the barn," Ethan commanded, sending his wolfhound up the rocks to round up the strays. He then bent down next to the boy and gently reached out to touch the blood at the back of Alana's head. Her eyes were closed and he wasn't really sure that she wasn't dead.

Emotions surged through him. Part of him wanted to pull her into his arms and protect her from everyone and everything, including nature. But another part of him wanted nothing to do with her ever again. Either way, he couldn't leave her here when she was hurt and stranded in the midst of a bad snow storm.

He leaned closer, pushing his face up next to hers to feel her warm breath on his cheek. That told him she was still alive. He sighed in relief, having feared the worst. A chill ran through his body, making him wonder if it was from the cold or from being so close to the deceitful girl who left him stranded at the altar. Funny how now she was in a similar position, being stranded instead. No matter how he felt, it didn't matter right now. He would help her, even if part of him could never forgive her for what she did.

"Is she dead?" asked Caleb, checking on his pine marten that was nestled in the canvas bag slung across his shoulder.

"Nay, but she is hurt. We need to get her back to the castle anon." Ethan reached out for her, but the boy stopped him.

"Nay! I'll take her," he said, stepping in front of him, blocking him from Alana. "No one is allowed inside the castle walls."

"Ye'll take her?" Ethan raised a brow. The boy wasn't still a child, but neither was he yet a man. He was so thin and that he didn't look to have enough muscles to pick up a log let alone a woman, and get her back to the castle by himself. "Nay, I'll do it. And dinna try to fight me, lad. The storm is gettin' worse. Do ye have a horse we can ride?"

"I've got a horse in the barn," Finn answered. The winds were getting so strong that it was going to be a chore just to get back to the castle.

Trapper barked and chased the sheep, sending them running.

"The dog did it!" cried Finn. "Let me open the gate and get them inside the barn." He took off at a run to finish the chore.

"So ye really did see Alana here after all," said Caleb, looking down at her.

"I told ye I wasna crazy," said Ethan. "Caleb, take the boy with ye on the other horse. I'll ride with Alana on this one. We need to get back to the castle and out of the storm. She's hurt, so we need to move quickly."

"But what are they doin' here?" asked Caleb. "And where have they been for the past five years?"

"I dinna ken but I intend to find out. But right now, we have to get them out of the storm."

"Aye," said Caleb as Ethan lifted Alana in his arms. Caleb helped him get Alana atop the horse.

Several minutes later, they were all headed for the castle with Trapper leading the way. The snow and rain came down so heavily that they had to travel slowly or risk a horse breaking a leg since they could barely see where they were going.

"Open the gate!" shouted Finn as they approached the castle.

"Ye really live here?" asked Caleb from the horse he shared with the boy. "I wouldna live here if I were a ghost." Caleb glanced over to Ethan when he said it. Ethan just moaned.

"Save yer breath," he warned his friend, not in the mood for teasing.

Trapper barked, running ahead of them, sneaking under the gate before it was even raised.

"Finn? Who is with ye?" growled one of the guards

hurrying down from the battlements to join them. Ethan recognized the man as the one who had threatened to shoot him with an arrow the last time he was here.

"Ye!" growled Ethan, drawing his sword at the same time the guard pulled his sword from the sheath.

"Alana! What happened?" A frantic woman ran out from the keep followed by the little girl that Ethan had seen atop the battlements. "Is she hurt?"

"Kirstine?" said Ethan, recognizing Alana's younger sister.

"Hello, Ethan," said the girl, flashing him a quick smile.

Ethan's gaze traveled down to the large bump sticking out from under the girl's cloak. She looked to be very pregnant.

Alana moaned and stirred in Ethan's arms as they sat atop the horse.

OPENING HER EYES, Alana realized she was on a horse with a man's arms wrapped around her. Kirstine stood next to them looking worried. Graeme walked up with his sword drawn.

"I'm no' here to fight," said the man on the horse with her. "I'm only here because Alana was hurt and I wanted to bring her home."

Alana stiffened in the man's arms. Her hand went to her aching head and she slowly turned to see him, knowing who it was before she even looked. She could never forget the deep timbre of Ethan MacKeefe's voice. Sure enough, it was Ethan who had helped her and brought her back to the castle. Being in his protective hold made her feel things she hadn't felt since the day she left him so long ago.

"Ethan," she whispered, her eyes momentarily interlocking with his before his glance turned back to Graeme.

"Graeme, put away yer sword," Alana commanded. "This is Ethan MacKeefe and he means us no harm." Alana knew Graeme wouldn't give her trouble since he was a friend of her family. Thankfully, Diarmad and his cronies weren't here right now or there would be a fight at hand.

"That's right," agreed Ethan. "My friend, Caleb, and I had just gotten to the isle when we realized our help was needed." He slipped off the horse and held out his arms to assist Alana.

Alana hesitated, her eyes darting over to her sister for support. Kirstine watched, nodding slightly.

"Thank ye," said Alana, putting her hands on Ethan's broad shoulders as he lifted her off the horse and helped her to the ground. She was so close to him that she could smell the whisky on his breath and the scent of pine clinging to his clothes. Memories flooded her mind of how she had always loved his scent as well as being warm and protected in his strong arms. She really missed this.

"They helped us get the sheep into the barn, too," stated Finn, jumping off the horse and running over to them. Caleb dismounted and held on to the reins of the horse as he came to join them.

"Well, thank ye much," said Alana, feeling disturbed that Ethan and Caleb were inside the castle walls. It was too risky. If they stayed too long, Diarmad might return. Plus, they were going to ask questions that she didn't want to answer.

The wind picked up and the snow fell faster. The storm was not letting up at all.

"Finn, take the horses to the barn and wipe them down," instructed Alana.

"Aye," he said, taking the reins of the horses. "But how will

Ethan and Caleb get back to their boat? It's goin' to be too hard to trek down the hill on foot in this storm."

The wolfhound lay down at Ethan's feet and put its nose down between its paws.

"They canna stay," said Albert, hurrying down from the battlements to join them. "Alana, they shouldna be inside the walls of Blackbriar Castle."

"Ye're right," agreed Alana, getting a stern look from her sister. "Ethan, I'm sorry, but ye'll have to leave now."

"Leave?" Ethan chuckled. "Alana, I didna think even someone as cold-hearted as ye could turn away a man who has just saved yer life. The storm is bad and we canna sail until it lets up or we're at risk of capsizin'."

"That's true. It's too dangerous to be out on the water now," agreed Caleb.

Isobel rushed over to Alana with her doll held tightly in one hand. She yanked on Alana's cloak, her eyes fastened to Ethan as she spoke.

"This is the man I saw atop the wall," said the little girl.

"Aye, that's right," answered Alana. "But he doesna belong here, sweetie."

"Mathair, please let him stay," begged the girl.

"Mathair?" Ethan's eyes shot up and interlocked with Alana's. Her body stiffened and her heart almost stopped beating. "Alana . . . ye have a daughter?" His words were laced with shock as well as disappointment. She wasn't sure what to say.

Her arm went around her daughter and she pulled the little girl closer. The snow continued to fall and the wind was becoming relentless. She wanted to tell Ethan the truth about Isobel, but she couldn't. Her father told her she had to keep it a secret, and he was probably right. If Ethan knew he had a child, he would never leave. She needed him to go back to the mainland before Diarmad returned or he might be killed.

The hurt in Ethan's eyes said everything that Alana had been feeling in her heart. She looked over to Kirstine once more, and her sister nodded. Alana felt so confused and her head ached from her fall. Her body shivered and she couldn't think straight. She remained silent instead of answering.

"Come, Caleb, I think it's time for us to leave after all," said Ethan, turning around. His dog jumped up and followed.

"Now?" asked Caleb, pulling his cloak tighter around him to ward off the chill. "But we havena found the doll yet."

"I no longer care," grumbled Ethan, walking faster toward the gate.

"The clan isna goin' to be happy to have to listen to Sophie's cryin' because we didna find her doll," protested Caleb, hurrying after Ethan.

"Mathair," said Isobel, tugging on Alana's cloak. When Alana looked down at her daughter, Isobel was holding up her doll. "This is my friend, Sophie's doll."

"It is?" Alana knew now where the doll had come from, and she wasn't happy about it. "Isobel, did ye sneak out of the castle to play with Osla's daughter, Sophie, after ye were told no' to?"

"I'm sorry," said Isobel, looking down and cradling the doll. "Finn used to take me there. He said it was all right."

"Well, Finn is goin' to have to answer for this later."

"Alana, ye canna mean to really let him leave," whispered Kirstine, hurrying to Alana's side.

"Well, it's no' like I can ask him to stay," Alana whispered back.

71

"Why no'?" asked Isobel, looking up at Alana with inno-cent eyes. "Ethan is nice. I like him."

Alana exchanged glances once more with Kirstine and let out a deep sigh. Her head hurt like the devil and she was so cold now that her teeth were chattering. But her heart longed for Ethan and she couldn't just let him walk out of her life now. Not before she could apologize for walking out of his life five years ago.

"Ethan," she called out, leaving the others, picking up her skirts and running after her ex-lover. "Ethan, I've changed my mind. I want ye to stay."

He stopped in his tracks so abruptly that she crashed into the back of him. When she stepped away, he turned to face her. Caleb stood next to him, watching them intently.

"What did ye say?" asked Ethan.

"I said . . . I want ye to stay." Her heart drummed relent-lessly in her chest. Once again, her eyes interlocked with his. His big, round brown eyes reminded her so much of Isobel's eyes that it made her want to cry.

"Ye want me to stay?"

Alana nodded slowly. "For now. Until the storm lets up and ye are able to sail back to the mainland."

"Aye, I'd like to stay and get warm by the fire," said Caleb, reaching out to pet the nose of his pine marten that was sticking its head out of his bag. "Slink would appreciate it, too."

"I dinna ken," Ethan answered in a low voice. "I dinna like to be around people who dinna want me and who've betrayed me."

Alana knew exactly what he was talking about, but she

couldn't address the issue. Not now with so many people watching and listening. It would have to wait.

"Please, Ethan," she said in a half-whisper, her fingers going to the wound on her head. She felt extremely light-headed and it was getting hard to think. "I – I need to . . ." She stopped speaking as blackness covered her eyes and her knees buckled beneath her. The last thing she remembered was Ethan reaching out to catch her before she hit the ground.

CHAPTER 5

"Quickly, we need to get her inside and out of the storm," commanded Ethan, gathering up Alana just before she crumpled to the ground.

"This way," said Kirstine, waving her arm, leading them into the keep.

"I dinna like this. Ye shoudna be here," growled the guard that Alana had called Graeme.

"Believe me, I dinna intend to stay," Ethan answered, following the small procession inside the keep and out of the storm. "As soon as I ken that Alana is all right and the storm lets up, I'm leavin'."

"Put her in her solar," said Kirstine. "It's this way."

Ethan followed the pregnant woman into a solar and gently laid Alana atop the bed. Her face was pale and the gash on her head looked deep. Trapper laid his chin on the bed and whined sadly.

"She's goin' to need stitches," said Ethan, tearing off the bottom of his leine and wrapping it around Alana's head. "Call for the healer."

"We dinna have a healer." Kirstine grabbed a bag and rushed back to the bed. "I will do it."

"Ye? Have ye done this before?" Ethan stood up and perused the woman.

"I can do it," she said, pulling a needle and thread out of her bag.

Ethan waited for her to say something else to him, but she didn't. Why had he somehow expected her to apologize for Alana leaving him at the altar? Even if not, a simple *I'm sorry for what my sister put ye through*, would have been appreciated.

Several servants followed them into the room.

"Finn, bring me a rag and water to clean her wound. Hurry," said Kirstine.

"Aye," answered the boy, rushing to the washstand.

"Why are ye all here at Blackbriar?" asked Ethan curiously. "And how long have ye been here?"

"I'm goin' to have to ask ye to leave the room now," said Kirstine, ignoring his questions altogether. "All of ye will have to leave while I sew up Alana's wound."

"Is Alana's husband in the castle?" asked Ethan, not knowing if he wanted to stay if the man who stole Alana from him was here. There had never been talk of Alana having another lover, but if she left him at the altar and had a daughter, it was apparent that it was so. If Ethan ever saw the man, he'd probably want to kill him for taking away the only girl he'd ever loved.

"I dinna have a da," said the little girl named Isobel, crawling atop the bed with the doll in her hand.

Ethan wickedly felt relief that he wasn't going to have to meet the man who bedded Alana and sired her daughter. By the little girl's remark, it sounded as if he were dead, and somehow Ethan didn't care. Still, his heart went out to the girl for her loss. His eyes fastened to the doll she held, and Sophie's sad wailing echoed in his head.

Isobel might not have a father, but Sophie didn't have a father or a mother. Her pain had to be worse. Ethan needed to get the doll from Isobel because that was the only thing that was going to bring comfort to the little girl back at the MacKeefe camp. But now that he knew Isobel no longer had a father, he didn't have the heart to take the doll from her. He was in a precarious predicament and wasn't sure what to do.

"I see," said Ethan, feeling like a black-hearted devil for not only feeling satisfaction knowing the man who stole his bride had passed away, but also for contemplating stealing from a child. What was the matter with him? Soon, he'd be no better than Alana's no-good father who stole the MacKeefe's herd on his daughter's wedding day. "I'll be in the great hall waitin' to hear about Alana's state," said Ethan, turning and walking to the door with his dog following. He couldn't stay in this room a moment longer.

"I'm sure Alana will be all right. She's a strong lass and a survivor," Kirstine said from behind him. "Now, everyone out, so I can get to work."

As Ethan and Caleb exited the room, Isobel ran up and tugged on Ethan's wet cloak.

"My name is Isobel," she told Ethan. "And my dolly's name is Annabelle."

"Well, hello, Isobel," said Ethan. "And also Annabelle," he said, smiling and nodding at the doll. "I'm Ethan, and I'm glad we've finally been properly introduced. Can ye show me how to get to the great hall?"

"And also, where we can get some food?" added Caleb, rubbing his belly.

"Sure I can." She surprised Ethan by reaching out and taking his hand. Her hand was so little and frail that he was afraid he'd smash it or break her bones with his rugged, strong grip. He had to be careful around her. "I like ye," said the girl with a wide smile, admiring Ethan. Part of him felt happy that Alana's daughter liked him. But another part of him felt sick. Did he really want the admiration of a child that was another man's but should have been his? It hurt to think what a child created by him and Alana might have looked like. He could only wonder if they would have had a son, or mayhap a daughter as cute as Isobel.

"Well . . . I . . . I like ye, too," said Ethan, figuring he was going to have to win the girl over if he was going to talk her into giving up the doll. He felt awful about all this. But if he went back to the MacKeefe camp without the doll, Hawke and the others were going to have his head.

"Is that the doll we're lookin' for?" asked Caleb in a mere whisper as they headed away to the great hall.

"Aye, I think so," Ethan answered, feeling like such a traitor as he held the hand of the girl and led her to the great hall like he was leading a lamb to slaughter.

"Ye're no' really goin' to take it from her, are ye?" asked Caleb.

"It's no' hers," he answered softly so the girl couldn't hear him. "It's Sophie's doll and Isobel is naught but a little thief."

"Well, what are we goin' to do about it?" asked Caleb.

"I dinna ken yet, but we'll come up with somethin'," answered Ethan, already devising a plan to get the doll and get the hell out of there before he had to deal with another ghost – this time a ghost of his troubled past.

* * *

When Alana's eyes flickered open, she saw Ethan holding her daughter's hand as they left the room. "Nay!" she blurted out, sitting up quickly, wanting to go after them.

"Lay down, Alana," commanded Kirstine, holding up a threaded needle. "I need to sew up the gash on yer head. But I'll never be able to do it if ye willna stay still."

Terrible pain shot through Alana's head and she suddenly dizzied. "Kirstine, Ethan is takin' Isobel away from me. Ye've got to stop him!"

"Nonsense," answered Kirstine. "No one is takin' her, now stop all yer fussin'. They are only goin' to the great hall to wait for word that ye are all right. Now, let me sew up that wound before ye bleed to death."

"Ooooh," moaned Alana, laying her cheek on the pillow so her sister could sew up the gash at the back of her head.

"Here, ye'd better have a swig of this." Kirstine held out a goat's bladder filled with liquid.

"What's in it?" she asked, sitting up and bringing it to her lips.

"I dinna ken. The man named Caleb that is with Ethan must have left it here. I think it is whisky. Drink some so ye willna feel the pain when I pierce yer flesh."

With one sip, Alana's throat caught afire and she could barely breathe. She gasped for air, her hand clutching her throat.

"What's the matter?" asked Kirstine, becoming alarmed.

Her eyes opened wide as well as her mouth. "It's tainted! God's eyes, I swear I didna ken!"

"It's no' tainted. That's . . . Mountain Magic." Alana was barely able to squeak out her raspy reply. "I'd ken it anywhere. Ethan and his friends used to drink it all the time."

"Mountain Magic?" asked Kirstine. "Och, I remember now. It's that hellfire potion brewed by the auld man of the MacKeefe Clan." She pulled it away and took a sniff before corking up the bladder and pushing it aside. "Ye'd better no' have anymore. Ye're already passin' out and this isna goin' to help."

"Kirstine, what am I goin' to do?" asked Alana, wincing in pain as her sister sewed up her wound.

"About what?"

"About Ethan."

"I dinna ken, but I heard him say he's leavin' as soon as the storm lets up."

"Nay," said Alana, her heart about breaking. After not seeing him for so many years, she didn't want him to leave, even though she knew it was risky to let him stay.

"I suppose it's for the best, Alana. Ye ken that if Diarmad finds them here, he'll probably kill them."

"Well, that's no longer acceptable. I canna send Ethan away. No' before I have a chance to talk to him. We still have time. Diarmad willna be back before the storm passes. I'm goin' to ask Ethan to stay," said Alana, trying to get out of bed.

"Stay still! I'm tryin' to close yer wound," scolded Kirstine. "And ye are in no shape to be goin' anywhere. There," she said, tying off the knot and snipping the thread. "Now, ye stay in bed. I'll have food brought to yer room."

"Nay, I canna do that! I have things to tend to, includin' takin' care of my daughter. Plus, I need to talk to Ethan. I have to explain to him why I left him." She threw her legs over the side of the bed and almost blacked out again. "Och," she said, her hand going to her head. Her stomach became queasy. "Mayhap I will take a wee nap first."

"Here, take another swig of this." Kirstine handed her the Mountain Magic. "It'll help ye sleep."

Since the pain throbbing in her head was more intense than being stuck with a needle, Alana gladly took the pouch and downed a big dram of the potent brew. She made a face as it burned a path down to her belly.

"Dinna let anyone tell Ethan a word about anythin'," she warned, her speech becoming slurred. Alana lay back on the bed and closed her eyes. "Especially, dinna let him ken he's Isobel's faither."

"I willna be the one to tell him that, but I think ye should." Kirstine got up and put away her supplies, wiping off her hands.

"Do ye really think so?" she asked, her eyes closing as the effects of the whisky took control of her body.

"I'll keep him here until ye awake, but then ye need to tell him somethin'," said Kirstine. "This canna go on any longer."

Kirstine was right, but the thought scared Alana out of her mind. It was going to be bad enough trying to explain to Ethan why she'd left him at the altar. But as hard as that was going to be, telling him he sired a child that she kept a secret for so long was going to be so much worse.

* * *

"WHERE IS EVERYONE?" Ethan asked as the small entourage

entered the great hall. The castle was vast, the room cold and dreary. A small fire flickered in the hearth across the room, barely large enough to create any warmth at all. But then again, the room was nearly void of people so mayhap it didn't matter.

"Dinna ask questions," grumbled Graeme, walking across the room to talk with the other guard named Albert.

"This place is kind of . . . eerie," said Ethan, feeling the chill of the dimly-lit vast chamber like icy fingers running up his spine.

"We dinna have many people livin' here," Finn told them. "And the – the laird doesna like us to use a lot of wood."

"What kind of laird would run a castle this way?" asked Ethan, glancing up at a hole in the roof where the snow was blowing in. The tapestries on the walls were torn and dirty, and a broken metal fixture that held candles dangled from the ceiling, all the candles stubs too small to burn. "Look at this place. It's in such disrepair that it is fallin' down around us. No wonder it's said to be haunted." He kicked at the stale, dirty rushes on the floor and part of the floor splintered up with it.

"It's no' haunted," said little Isobel, looking up at him with wide, brown eyes.

"Aye, it is," said Finn, shooting the girl a nasty glare. "Isobel, mayhap ye should go to bed now."

"Nay! I want to stay with Ethan. He's nice." The little girl stuck out her tongue at Finn.

"Would ye like an ale?" asked a serving wench, handing Caleb and Ethan each a mug.

"Ale? Nay, I've got somethin' better," said Caleb, reaching to his side and then looking around the floor. "What happened to the bladder of Mountain Magic I had tied to my waist?" he asked.

"Ye probably forgot it on the boat," said Ethan with a scowl. "Ye're always forgettin' things."

"Nay, I'm sure I had it with me," Caleb protested.

"Then mayhap that little thief stole it," remarked Ethan, talking about Caleb's pine marten but, for some reason, Isobel thought he meant her.

"I'm sorry I took it," she admitted with a pout. "I left it in the room for my mathair."

"Ye took it?" asked Caleb in surprise, still patting his side as if he thought it was going to magically reappear.

"Isobel!" cried Finn, looking up at the men as if he were expecting them to be angry or perhaps beat the girl for what she did.

"Isobel? Ye stole the flask of whisky from Caleb and he never even kent it?" asked Ethan with a chuckle, thoroughly amused.

"I said I'm sorry," she said. Her bottom lip stuck out in a pout as if she were going to cry. She hugged her doll tightly to her chest. "Annabelle told me to do it."

"Annabelle told ye to do it?" Ethan eyed up the girl. "Then mayhap Annabelle should be punished."

"Nay!" she cried, hugging the doll. "Annabelle is my best friend now since Sophie is gone."

"Isobel, quiet," scolded Finn. "Yer mathair is goin' to be angry when she finds out what ye're tellin' him."

"Why couldna she play with Sophie?" asked Ethan, not understanding what was going on. "There doesna seem to be any other children on the isle that I can tell."

"I – I think I'd better light the candles. It's gettin' very dark." Finn took off at a half-run in the opposite direction.

"There's somethin' odd goin' on around here," Caleb told Ethan.

"I agree," answered Ethan. "After all, ye are one of the stealthiest people I ken. If ye had yer flask of whisky stolen by a child, then ye must have had yer mind elsewhere."

"Perhaps my mind was preoccupied with other things," said Caleb, his eyes taking in the entire gloomy room. Slink poked his head out of Caleb's pouch just then and Isobel started giggling.

"What is that?" The girl's eyes filled with amusement as she pointed to Caleb's pet.

"This? Oh, this is my friend, Slink," said Caleb, pulling the long, rodent-like animal from his pouch and holding it out to her. "Would ye like to pet him?"

"All right," said the little girl, petting his back gingerly with one finger. "Can I hold him?"

"Ye can, but ye're goin' to need two hands to do it. And we should sit down at the table so ye dinna drop him," explained Caleb.

"All right," she agreed. "Ethan, can ye watch Annabelle for me while I hold Slink?" The girl handed the doll to Ethan.

"Sure," he said blindly, clutching the doll as Caleb and the girl headed over to the trestle table.

Ethan looked at the doll in his hand, not able to believe his sudden luck. This was the answer to all the MacKeefes' problems. Or, at least, it was the answer for all of them finally getting a good night's sleep. Well, this was going to be easier than he thought. All he had to do now was leave here with the doll, get on the boat, and sail back to the MacKeefe camp. He stuck the doll under his cloak and wandered over to the trestle table where Isobel was giggling and petting Slink on her lap.

"Pssst," said Ethan, trying to get Caleb's attention. Caleb was laughing and looked up. Ethan opened his cloak and nodded toward the doll. Caleb's smile disappeared.

"Isobel, can ye go to the kitchen and ask the cook if he has anythin' my pine marten can eat?" asked Caleb.

"I will," said the little girl, so excited that she ran off without even remembering to take the doll.

Caleb picked up his pet and headed over to Ethan.

"Here," said Ethan, handing him the doll. "Take it and let's get the hell out of here."

"But that's Isobel's doll," said Caleb, looking down at it but doing nothing to take it from him. "Dinna ye think she is goin' to miss it?"

"No' if we leave before she finds out. Besides, it's really Sophie's doll. And if Sophie didna say a thing about givin' it to Isobel, then it's most likely that little thief stole it from her just like she pilfered yer Mountain Magic. Now, take it and let's get back to the boat."

"Me take it?" Caleb shook his head so furiously that his black curly hair bounced around his shoulders. "Nay," he said, holding up a halting hand. "I'm no' the one that's goin' to be stealin' from a child."

"We arena stealin' it. We're . . . returnin' it to its proper owner, that's all."

"Nay, Ethan. I willna do it! Ye carry the doll. I dinna want to be a part of any of this deceit."

"It's too late," said Ethan in a low voice. "Ye're already part of it, like it or no'. Now take the doll and let's get movin'. I canna stand another night of hearin' Sophie cry."

"That bothers ye, does it?" Caleb petted his pine marten and raised his chin.

"Aye, it does."

"And what about when Isobel starts cryin' that her doll is gone? Will that bother ye, too?"

"No' if I am back at the MacKeefe camp and canna hear it. Now take it!" He smashed the rag doll up against Caleb's chest, but Caleb wouldn't take it. Instead, he stubbornly crossed his arms over his chest, still cradling his pine marten in the crook of his arm. Ethan let go of the doll and turned quickly, hearing a soft thud as the doll fell to the ground and landed in the rushes.

"What are ye doin' to Annabelle?" Isobel stood staring at Ethan with her mouth wide open. Her eyes went to the doll lying on the floor in the dirty rushes.

"I . . . I . . . I dropped her?" said Ethan, already kicking himself for not sounding like he meant it. "I'm sorry," he apologized, feeling terrible now for trying to take her doll, even though she was the one who gave it to him in the first place.

"Ye were tryin' to steal her from me!" Isobel bent down and picked up the doll, kissing it and clutching it to her chest. "Ye are a mean man." Tears formed in her eyes.

"Nay, I'm no' mean," Ethan tried to convince her, but it didn't change her mind.

"I hate ye!" cried the little girl, going from loving and admiring him to wanting nothing to do with him in just a few minutes.

"Isobel, wait." Ethan reached out for the girl, but when he took her by the arm, she leaned over and bit him on the hand.

"Och! Bid the devil what did ye do that for?" Ethan released her and rubbed his hand while Caleb chuckled from behind him.

"Aye, ye really have a way with children, just like ye told Hawke. I can see that, now," commented Caleb.

"I never want to see ye again!" Isobel turned and ran from the room crying.

"Ye ken, it seems to me ye have an ill effect on girls," said Caleb, walking up next to him.

"What do ye mean?" Ethan watched the girl fleeing the great hall, wondering how he was going to fix this mess he was in.

"Well, accordin' to my calculations, isna this the second time a girl has left ye standin' here, never wantin' to see ye again? First it was Alana, and now it's her daughter."

Ethan felt a sinking sensation in his chest to realize this was true. "Aye, I guess so," he said, wondering where he went wrong. This time, instead of Alana leaving him, it was her little daughter. Either way, both times hurt.

"I think it's time we leave," said Ethan, wanting to go as quickly as possible. The longer he stayed, the more chance there was that he was going to offend someone else.

"But it's still stormin' out there," complained Caleb, petting his pine marten. "Slink doesna care for the rain and snow and neither do I. Plus, we're both hungry. I've yet to get warm or to find anythin' to eat around here."

"Oh, there ye two are," said Kirstine, entering the great hall and waddling over to them, rubbing her belly.

"How is Alana?" asked Ethan, genuinely concerned for her health.

"I closed up her wound and she is sleepin' soundly. She'll be feelin' much better come mornin'."

"Guid. Then we'll be on our way."

"So soon?" asked Kirstine, stepping in their path so they had to stop. "Look. Here comes the food now."

Ethan turned to find two servants carrying platters of food into the room. His stomach growled. He was so hungry that right now he'd eat a rat and not complain.

"We're stayin'. Right, Ethan?" asked Caleb with wishful longing in his eyes, staring at the piping-hot food. His tongue shot out and he licked his lips as the servant came closer.

"Come, sit down and eat," offered Kirstine. "And warm yer bones and dry yer clothes by the fire. Finn," she called to her brother. "Throw some more logs on the fire. It's cold in here."

"Really?" asked the boy. "But Diarmad doesna like us to burn too much wood."

"Well, he's no' here so he willna ken. It'll be all right for one night," explained Kirstine. "Now do it."

"Aye," said the boy, hurrying off to do the work.

"Diarmad?" Ethan raised a brow. "Who is that? Is he laird of the castle?"

"Aye," she answered, looking worried. "He is my . . . husband."

"I see," Ethan said, perusing the girl. She seemed frightened. "Where is yer faither, Gil Chisholm?" he asked. "Are yer parents livin' here as well?" He fired the questions at her quickly, eager to learn more.

"Well . . . uh . . . my faither is here," she said, sounding reluctant to answer.

"Guid. Lead me to him. I'd like to have a word with him,"

said Ethan, wanting to kill the man right now for everything he'd done.

"Nay, ye canna do that."

"Why no'?" asked Ethan.

"Because he is ill. He is sleepin' and canna be disturbed." Kirstine looked the other way when she answered. "Let's all sit down and eat before the food gets cold," she suggested.

Something wasn't right here, but Ethan decided he couldn't push the girl too hard or she'd tell him nothing. He'd eat for now and try to pump her for information later. "Caleb, I suppose a bite to eat and gettin' warm by the fire might no' be a bad idea after all," said Ethan.

"I agree!" Caleb smiled from ear to ear. Then his pine marten saw a mouse run by and jumped out of his arms to run after the rodent.

"But we're no' stayin' the night," added Ethan.

"We're no'?" asked Caleb looking quickly at Ethan and then back to the servant with the platter of food again.

"Ye're no'? Why no'?" asked Kirstine. "I think ye should. I'm sure Alana will want to see ye before ye go."

"I agree with her," said Caleb, reaching out and grabbing a leg of mutton from the servant's tray. "Do ye have any Mountain Magic by any chance?"

"Do ye mean this?" Kirstine held up Caleb's flask and Ethan took it from her.

"That'll do." Ethan lifted it to his mouth and took a swig. The burning sensation of the liquid trailed a path down his throat, making him feel more relaxed immediately.

"Let's all sit," said Kirstine, leading them up to the dais.

"Will Alana be joinin' us?" asked Ethan, taking another swig of the potent brew. "I'd like to talk to her."

"I'm sorry, but it'll have to wait until mornin'," said Kirstine. "My sister needs her rest. She's been through a lot today."

"Havena we all?" asked Ethan, taking another swig of whisky before Caleb leaned over and snatched it away from him.

"Ethan doesna want to stay here because he's afraid of the ghost," said Caleb, catching Ethan off guard.

"Haud yer wheesht, ye fool," Ethan said through gritted teeth. He'd almost forgotten about the ghost until Caleb just mentioned it.

"The ghost? What ghost?" By the way Kirstine batted her eyelids, Ethan knew she was keeping something from him.

"Have ye ever heard the scream of a woman from the tower window?" asked Ethan curiously.

"Nay." Kirstine busied herself putting food on her trencher. "Nay, I dinna believe so. What do ye mean?"

"It's nothin'," he told her, grabbing the flask back from Caleb. Something told him the girl was lying and he had no idea why. It was already proving to be a very long night.

CHAPTER 6

*E*than awoke during the night, having fallen asleep with his head down on a trestle table as he sat in front of the fire. His dog lay at his feet under the table. He'd had every intention of sailing the boat back to the MacKeefe camp and not staying the night, but the weather had been ruthless. Between Caleb and Kirstine, they'd convinced him not to go.

Part of him didn't really want to leave yet anyway. He needed to make sure Alana was going to be all right. Not to mention, he wanted to confront her about their past.

Through the dark, Ethan could see the embers on the hearth. The room was frigidly cold and snow still blew in through the hole in the roof. He decided to tend to the fire himself since he wasn't even sure where to find a servant right now. It was amazing that a castle of this size didn't have more occupants. Something was odd here, and he needed to find out more.

Stepping over Caleb sprawled out on the floor, Ethan made his way back to the entrance of the great hall. His wolfhound darted out from under the table and followed him into the courtyard. The moon was still high in the sky but Ethan could see a slight orange glow as the sun was just starting to rise on the horizon. The snow had stopped but it was nearly knee-deep in places and not easy to walk.

"Trapper, we've got to find a few logs for the fire," he told the dog, wandering across the courtyard in the snow. There didn't seem to be any guards on the battlements. As far as he could tell, he was the only one out here. The courtyard was oddly empty, bringing about the feeling of death. Back at Hermitage Castle there were always guards and servants milling about even in the wee hours of the morning. Then again, the MacKeefe's laird, Storm MacKeefe, would never allow the fire to get so low on such a cold day.

The MacKeefes were good people and there were quite a few of them. Here at Blackbriar Castle, the halls were nearly empty and the walls looked to be crumbling down around him. Nothing was cared for at all. Ethan wondered if old, crazy Mad Murdock was still alive and residing here, and also why Alana and her family were staying here at this horrible place at all. It was almost as if they were in hiding. He could understand why, since the Chisholm name was ill-regarded by most, thanks to the antics of Alana's father. But still, he didn't like this at all.

If this laird, Diarmad, allowed his castle to be in such disrepair, then he must not care about the people who lived here. Nothing was right, from the way no one acknowl-edged even seeing or hearing the ghost, to the little girl being kept away from other children. No wonder nobody set foot on this isle. There were a bunch of lunatics living here!

The dog whined and darted off, hopping through the snow, leading the way to a wooden enclosure filled with logs.

"Here we go," said Ethan, walking over to collect some wood. From his position, he could see the tower perfectly where he'd spotted the ghost. Looking upward, his mind must have been playing tricks on him because he thought he saw a dark shadow float over the battlements and then quickly disappear.

"I need to wake up, Trapper," he said to the dog, rubbing his eyes and blinking. He might have shaken off the whole thing if Trapper hadn't started growling lowly, looking up to the battlements as well. "Did ye see it, too, boy?" he asked, watching the dog lower its head, seeming to be able to see something that Ethan couldn't.

"What are ye talkin' about?" came a feminine voice from behind the woodpile.

Ethan turned back to see Alana standing behind the structure with an armload of logs.

"Alana." His heart skipped a beat seeing her. He tried to push aside the feelings he still held for her, but it wasn't easy. Then he thought about how she'd played him for a fool, and his loving thoughts of his past betrothed were quickly buried once again. "What are ye doin' out here? Ye should be in bed."

"In bed? Hah! Someone's got to get the logs for the fire before we all freeze to death." She took a step and lost her balance in the deep snow, losing her grip. The logs clattered to the ground. She would have landed on her rump if Ethan hadn't reached out and caught her.

"Careful," he said, putting his hands under her arms and helping her to stand.

. . .

ONCE AGAIN, Alana reveled in the feeling of being in Ethan MacKeefe's arms. Why did it affect her so much after all this time?

"Thank ye," she said, looking up at him as she regained her footing. Just being in his presence brought back so many wonderful memories that, for a brief moment, she was transported back to the past. Back to the days when life was good and she looked forward to a future with Ethan.

Ethan's slight smile warmed her as he reached out and brushed the snow off the front of her cloak. It was an innocent action, and she was sure he only meant to help her, but she felt a tingle of excitement flit through her when his hand came close to her breast.

"Ye are injured and should be restin'," he told her, sounding genuinely concerned. She had thought he'd be furious with her, but if he was, he kept his emotions in control.

"Nay. The castle is cold and I want to stock the hearth before everyone awakes."

"Ye?" He bent down to collect the logs she'd dropped, looking up at her as he spoke. "Shouldna the servants be doin' this work instead?"

She couldn't tell him that the servants were prisoners of Diarmad's as well and that she usually didn't ask them to do things when Diarmad was away. She felt sorry for them and wanted to help them in any way she could.

"Even servants deserve a day to sleep a little later than normal," she answered, hoping he wouldn't ask more. How could she tell him that everyone at Blackbriar Castle was a prisoner and that they weren't even given a boat so they were stranded on the isle?

"Alana," he said, sounding very serious as he stood and

arranged the logs in his arms. Trapper wandered off to sniff around, lifting his leg on the side of a wooden cart. "Why did ye do it?" he asked.

She knew what he meant but wasn't ready to answer.

"I told ye, I do it to help out the servants." Picking up her skirts she took a step in the snow but he moved in front of her to block her way.

"Ye ken what I mean. How could ye leave me standin' alone on our weddin' day? I thought . . . I thought ye loved me."

Seeing the hurt in his eyes, she wanted nothing more than to pull him to her and kiss him and tell him she'd never stopped loving him, not even once over the last five years. But if she did that, it would only make more questions arise. Ones she couldn't answer.

"I'm sorry," she whispered, staring directly into his eyes. "I never meant to hurt ye, Ethan. Ye have to believe that it's true."

"Well ye did hurt me. Deeply. I loved ye with all my heart, Alana. I was lookin' forward to spendin' the rest of my life with ye."

"I ken. Me, too." She had wanted that more than anything. It was a dream she'd had since she was a young girl. Alana had always been in love with Ethan, long before he even knew it. They would have had a good life together as husband and wife if her father hadn't called for her to help him. At the time, she thought it was a temporary thing and that her mother would be rescued quickly. Then, she'd hoped to be able to come back to Ethan. But after she realized they were tricked and framed, everything changed. When her mother was killed, and all of them were taken captive, life had taken a horrible turn. She had hoped to find a way to make things right again but, unfortunately, that never happened.

Life isn't always fair, she realized. She'd had no other choice at the time because she would do anything to help her family. Alana had held hope in her heart of someday being back with Ethan but, still, she was no closer to returning to the man she loved.

"Alana, look at me and tell me that ye never really loved me. Tell me and I'll leave here and never bother ye again." He shifted the logs to one arm and touched her shoulder with the other.

Alana squeezed her eyes closed, feeling her body tremble. She couldn't say she'd never loved him. Not when all she wanted to say was that she never wanted to leave, and that she never dreamed she'd be in such a horrible situation. If Ethan knew about the smuggling, he would turn in her father who'd be put to death. Albert, Graeme, and the others who were naught more than pawns in this deceitful game would be punished or killed as well, she was sure of it. And she had no idea what would happen to her siblings, herself, or her daughter. Was this a chance she was willing to take?

She couldn't let him know what was going on here. Not now, not like this.

Opening her eyes, she spied Albert and Graeme watching her from the guardhouse. While they were her friends, they still took orders from Diarmad. By having Ethan here, she was putting them at risk as well. Perhaps it would be better for all involved if Ethan left the isle.

"Say it," growled Ethan, tempting her to do what she knew would send him and his friend off the isle, never to return. If he thought she didn't want him, he would do nothing to try to save her. With them gone, the secret would be safe once again. She wouldn't have to worry. Or would she? Because if she never saw Ethan again, she didn't know if she could live with that either. Mayhap, instead, she should be asking for his help like her sister said. Right now, she was so confused that she didn't know what to do at all.

"Are ye married, Ethan?" she asked, needing to know.

"Nay. When ye left me, ye took with ye a piece of my heart. I couldna love another."

"Really?" she asked in a mere whisper, feeling her heart breaking. It was one thing that her love life was doomed by her decision, but she'd never meant to intentionally ruin his life as well. "So ye . . . ye dinna have a wife or . . . or any bairns." She couldn't keep looking into his eyes when she said it, and instead she looked at the ground.

The gentle feel of his fingers lifting her chin had her heart fluttering once again as she now looked deeply into his eyes when he answered.

"Nay," he said in a whisper. "I had always thought we would someday have bairns together. I had always hoped that someday ye'd come back to me even though there were times I hated ye so much I swore I never wanted to see ye again. I waited for ye to return, Alana. I waited and wished and dreamed that we could someday still be together. But ye never returned."

His words about made her cry. She felt the tears welling up and tried desperately to hold them back. Her lips trembled as his eyes turned to her mouth and he leaned forward to kiss her. She wanted this more than anything right now. Alana craved the feel of Ethan's lips against hers. He lifted her mouth to his and their lips touched, sending a spark of desire through her. As the kiss continued, she reached out and put her hands on his chest. Warmth flowed through her and her entire body came back to life. It was a kiss of hope and of promise. This is what she needed to pull herself out of the dark place she was in and to find that light in her life once again. Their lips slowly parted and she thought they'd kiss again but, instead, this time he pulled away from her.

"Nay," he said in a low voice. "This is no' right. Ye didna wait for me, Alana," came his angry growl. "Ye tricked me and played me for a fool, and I canna forget it."

"What?" Her eyes popped open. "Nay, that's no' true," she protested, shaking her head.

He dropped his hand from her chin and with it went all the warmth that had filled her moments before.

"Isna it? Ye ran off with another man on the day of our weddin'. Ye were only at the MacKeefe camp to distract us, while yer faither stole our livestock and tried to sell it to the MacDougals. We almost had a battle over it, but luckily our laird kept peace between our clans. After that, ye left quickly and without even a simple guidbye."

"Ethan, it's no' like that! Ye've got it all wrong."

He didn't stop, he just kept on talking. "Ye birthed another man's baby – the baby that was supposed to be ours," he spat, sounding extremely disgusted. "And then ye hid here on this deserted isle for some godforsaken reason, probably livin' in fear and shame for treatin' me so bad."

"Is that what ye think?" she gasped. "Ethan, everythin' isna always just about ye." His assumptions irked her since he thought he was the only one who had been wronged.

"How auld is yer daughter, Alana? Four? Tell me," he ground out, demanding an answer.

"Well, aye, Isobel is four, but –"

"Och, I see it all clearly now," he spat.

"See what?" she asked, not sure what he meant.

"The bastard was beddin' ye all the while we were plannin' on being wed. When were ye goin' to tell me that ye were already pregnant with another man's child? And were ye ever in love with me at all, or was that all an act to get close to me so ye could steal from the MacKeefes?" Anger filled his dark brown eyes and he looked like he hated her now. Sadly, she couldn't blame him.

"Nay, Ethan, ye dinna understand."

"Nay, I dinna," he said, a sarcastic tinge to his voice. "So why dinna ye tell me the way it really is?"

"I – I –" She didn't know what to say. She saw Albert and Graeme rushing down the stairs of the battlements and trudging across the snow-laden courtyard toward them.

"Tell me!" he shouted, scaring her. Trapper heard him yell and came running over. The hound jumped up, putting its paws on Ethan's shoulders. "Get down!" snapped Ethan, dropping the logs and pushing the dog away.

"Ethan, please dinna hate me." Her eyes flashed over to the guards and then back to him. "I want to tell ye . . . everythin'. But I . . . I canna do that right now." Even if she did decide to come clean with him, she was sure Albert and Graeme would stop her from doing so. It was their job to keep this all a secret, and if word got back to Diarmad, they might be killed because of her. She couldn't let that happen.

"Canna or willna?" he asked, his words throwing down the gauntlet in challenge. "If ye have somethin' to say to all this, then ye'd better do it fast."

The wind picked up and Alana hugged herself to stay

warm, looking at the ground and not answering. Her lip trembled and she felt as if she wanted to cry. Albert and Graeme came closer.

"I thought I kent ye, Alana, but now I see that our time together meant nothin' to ye," continued Ethan.

"That's no' true," she said, following after him as he stormed back to the keep, trudging through the snow.

"What's goin' on here?" asked Graeme, his hand going to his sword as he quickly followed.

"There is nothin' at all goin' on here," Ethan answered, stopping and turning around. "Alana, all the promises we made to each other were nothin' but lies. I can see that now."

"Ye dinna ken what ye're sayin'." Alana was becoming more and more upset by Ethan's words. She was about to tell him everything but then Albert and Graeme glared at her and shook their heads in a silent reminder to keep quiet.

"I'm done with ye," spat Ethan, throwing his hands in the air and hurrying to the stairs to enter the great hall. "I'm done with all women," he complained under his breath, almost walking into Caleb who was hopping on one foot, putting on his boots as he walked out.

"Caleb, let's go," commanded Ethan.

"Go?" asked Caleb, standing up and running a hand through his hair as he yawned. He looked at Ethan and Alana and then the guards. "Go where?"

"We're leavin' for MacKeefe camp anon. Get yer belongin's and meet me at the boat."

"We're leavin'? Now? But it's barely light," complained Caleb, yawning again and squinting as he looked out at the lightening sky.

"Did I hear ye're leavin'?" Kirstine hurried over with Finn

at her side. "But ye just got here. Please dinna go yet. At least stay until ye break the fast."

"Aye, I could go for a boiled goose egg or mayhap a little brown bread and pottage," said Caleb, always wanting to eat.

"Nay. They need to leave," commanded Graeme.

"Thank ye for yer kindness, Kirstine, but I suddenly feel as if I dinna want to be here any longer," said Ethan. He glared at Alana over his shoulder when he said it.

"What's goin' on?" asked Kirstine, looking over at Alana.

Once again, Alana was put in an uncomfortable position. Isobel came down the stairs clutching her doll. She ran over and clung to Alana's skirts.

"What's the matter, sweetheart?" asked Alana, running a hand over her daughter's soft hair.

"I'm scared," said Isobel.

"Of the ghost?" asked Caleb.

The little girl shook her head. "Nay. Someone is tryin' to get Annabelle." She looked up at Ethan when she said it.

"Let's go, Caleb," said Ethan, not even responding to that.

"All right," grumbled Caleb, patting the pouch hanging at his side. "Wait, where's Slink?" He looked around the floor. "He was here a minute ago but now I canna find him."

"Egads," complained Ethan, whistling for his dog. Trapper bounded over and sat at Ethan's feet. "Trapper, find Slink," was all he said. The dog put its nose to the rushes and hurried back into the great hall with Caleb running after him. "I'll meet ye at the boat. And hurry!"

Ethan turned to go, but stopped in his tracks when little Isobel stepped toward him, handing him her doll.

"What are ye doin'?" asked Ethan, looking at the doll but not taking it.

"I think Annabelle wants to go back to Sophie," she said.

"Honey, are ye sure?" asked Alana.

"Aye, Mathair," she answered, still looking frightened. "She'll be safe there." Alana didn't understand. If the girl was afraid of Ethan, why was she giving him the doll? It made no sense to her at all.

"Nay. I dinna want it," said Ethan with a shake of his head.

"But Sophie will cry without Annabelle," said the girl. "Ye said so."

"Dinna worry about it. I'll get her another doll. It doesna matter."

"We'll see ye down to the boat," said Albert, wanting to make sure that Ethan left before Diarmad and the other men returned.

"Dinna bother. I think I can find the way myself," said Ethan.

"All right, I have Slink," said Caleb, walking out, sticking the pine marten into his pouch. "Although I think it's rude of us no' to stay to break the fast."

"Let's go," said Graeme, reaching out and grabbing Caleb's arm.

Ethan had his sword drawn before Alana knew what happened.

"It seems to me ye are in a big hurry to get rid of us," said Ethan. "Now, let go of my friend's arm before I have to make ye do it."

Albert's hand moved toward his sword as well. Alana realized she had to do something quickly before a fight broke out. She stepped in between the guard and Ethan. "I'm sure they are only tryin' to be helpful and mean ye and Caleb no harm." She turned and glared at the guards and shook her head.

Slowly, Graeme released Caleb's arm and nodded to Albert. Then the two of them turned and walked away.

"What's goin' on here, Alana?" asked Ethan. "I want the truth!"

"They are just protectin' me, that's all. Please, at least stay for somethin' to eat before ye leave."

"Aye," agreed Kirstine. "Plus, I have a basket of things we found left at the hut after Osla and the children left. They were Osla's things. Caleb told me she died. I thought perhaps now that she is gone, her children would like to have them."

"Oh," said Ethan, looking over at Caleb.

"It might be nice," said Caleb, running his hand over the back of his pet. "I mean, for Osla's children and all."

A woman walked by with a tray of food and Caleb's head turned to watch her. Trapper sat down at Ethan's feet and whined.

"Fine," he said. "We'll stay for a bite to eat, but we will leave as soon as the meal is finished."

Alana liked that Ethan was staying. She realized it would mean she had another chance to talk to him to try to explain things. This time, she decided she was going to tell him everything. Or at least whatever she could without putting anyone's life at stake.

"Och, I like that idea," said Caleb. "Let's go get somethin' to eat, Ethan." Caleb's eyes lit up more when a tray of leftover cold duck passed beneath his nose when another servant walked by with more food.

"Go on without me," said Ethan. "I'm no' hungry. Besides, I have somewhere else to go." Caleb hurried off, not having to be told twice.

"Ye have somewhere else to go?" Alana's brows raised. "Where?"

"The garderobe," he said, but Alana didn't believe him.

Ethan walked away, leaving Alana standing there with Kirstine.

"Diarmad will be back soon, so they'd better no' stay too long," warned Kirstine.

"I'm sure they willna," Alana answered, her eyes still fastened to Ethan's back. "Kirstine, I think I want to tell Ethan everythin.'"

"Do ye think it's wise?"

"If he understands what happened, then mayhap he willna hate me so much."

"But Faither willna be happy. Mayhap ye'd better clear it with him first. He'll ken what to do."

"Mayhap," she said. "Then again, mayhap Faither is the last person I want to listen to right now."

CHAPTER 7

"Caleb," said Ethan, joining his friend at the table a little while later.

"Have some food, Ethan. It's guid," answered Caleb, stuffing his mouth full of braised cabbage and roasted meat. He picked up his trencher and offered it to Ethan.

"Nay, I dinna want that," Ethan grumbled, his eyes scanning the room.

"All right, then mayhap Slink will want some instead." He held out a piece of cold duck to his pet that eagerly took it and dove under the table.

"Somethin's no' right here," said Ethan under his breath.

"I ken." Caleb licked off his fingers. "They really need to warm up the meat and add a sauce to it. But it's still guid this way, too. I dinna mind."

"No' that ye fool," snapped Ethan leaning closer to talk to Caleb so no one would hear them. "I pretended to take a walk to the garderobe, but I really checked out the rest of the castle. It seems this broken down place is nearly deserted just like I thought. I didna find another soul anywhere but in the great hall. Dinna ye think it is odd that a laird would take most of his men and leave the women and servants only protected by two guards?"

"No' really. After all, no one ever comes to this isle. Take us for instance – we didna even ken anyone lived here. I'd say that's the best protection," laughed Caleb, picking up his tankard and taking a swig of ale.

"Aye. But why do they want their presence here to be a secret?"

"They are probably in hidin' after Alana's faither wronged so many people. Mayhap we should turn them in. I ken a lot of clans that would be happy to get their hands on Gil Chisholm." Caleb continued eating. "Do ye think there is a reward?"

"I dinna like it. I feel as if Alana and the others fear somethin' or someone."

"Well, ye have been a little gruff with them, Ethan."

"No' me. I mean . . . I dinna ken, but somethin' is off. I'm goin' to sneak out of here again and check the rooms on the opposite side of the castle. I have a feelin' I might just find that coward, Gil Chisholm, hidin' somewhere. If I do, he's goin' to be a sorry man. I have a feelin' Alana is tryin' to protect him and that is why she is no' tellin' me things."

"Ye think Gil is hidin' from us?" Caleb asked a little too loudly.

"Keep yer voice down," warned Ethan. "I dinna believe for one minute he's no' watchin' us right now, plannin' on stealin' our boat or whatever he can get his hands on."

"Our boat?" Caleb looked up in concern. "If that happens, we'll be stranded here and have no way back to camp."

"Then I suggest we leave soon before he has a chance to plan anythin'."

"So what do ye want me to do?"

"I need ye to cause a distraction so I can slip away and look in the last few rooms outside the great hall before we go. I want to ken if her faither is here or no' before we leave. I've been told he is ill and restin', but I havena yet found him."

"If so, are ye goin' to turn him in for what he's done?"

"I think it's our duty, dinna ye?"

"But he's Alana's faither. Doesna that mean anythin' to ye?"

"Nay. No' anymore. Alana is nothin' to me but a traitor, just like her auld man. Now, hurry up and cause a distraction. I've got work to do."

"Now?" Caleb made a face and looked down to his trencher filled with food. "I am no' done eatin' yet. Besides, I wouldna ken how to make a distraction."

"Oh, aye, ye are finished." Ethan whistled for Trapper. The dog ran over to the table. "Go on, boy," said Ethan, getting up from the table and nodding to Caleb's trencher of food.

"Ethan, nay!" shouted Caleb, but it was too late. Trapper gladly put his paws on the table and started to devour Caleb's food. Caleb yelled, the dog barked, and Slink jumped up on the table making a hissing noise. One of the servant women screamed and dropped a platter of food before turning and running back to the kitchen. The two guards ran over to the dais as well as Kirstine and Finn.

"Now that's what I call a distraction," said Ethan proudly, getting up from the table. This was his chance. He slipped back into the shadows, and while the commotion was taking everyone's attention, he hurried down the corridor to look for Alana's father. He was about to turn and go in another direction when a door to a chamber opened. He jumped back and stood with his back against the wall peeking out from around a corner.

"I'll be back, Faither. Please get some sleep." It was Alana. She left the room and hurried back toward the great hall.

Ethan stepped around the corner, checking the hallway to make certain he hadn't been noticed. Then he quickly slipped inside the room that Alana had just exited, thankful the door was not locked. Stopping in his tracks, he laid eyes on a thin man sitting on the edge of the bed with his feet hanging over the side.

"Gil? Gil Chisholm?" he asked, thinking this man looked so thin and gaunt that it was hard to recognize him as the same man that was once almost his father-by-marriage.

"Who are ye?" The man's head snapped up and he looked at Ethan. "Ethan MacKeefe," he said under his breath, looking upset, quickly pulling a blanket over his legs. "What are ye doin' here?"

"I think the real question is what are ye doin' here?"

"What does it matter?"

"It matters because I think ye are in hidin', ye thief and traitor. Ye will pay for the things ye've done. I will make certain of it." His hand went to the hilt of his sword.

"Ye shouldna be on this isle at all. Ye must leave anon before it's too late."

"I'm no' leavin' before I get some answers." Ethan walked closer to the open window and glanced out. He thought for a moment he saw the mast of a ship disappearing behind the rocks on the far side of the isle, then decided he must be mistaken. The cliffs were too jagged and steep. There was nowhere to dock a boat on the west side of the Isle of Kerrera. "What is goin' on here?" he asked.

"There is nothin' happenin'."

"Why are ye even on this isle? And why are Alana and her siblin's here? This is no place for them. Especially no' for her young daughter."

His head snapped up at hearing that. "She told ye about her daughter?"

"Why arena ye all back with yer clan?"

"Ye ask too many questions, MacKeefe. Now, go back to yer camp and dinna return. I canna make my past mistakes right and neither can I bring back my dead wife who died because of me. I canna expect ye'll ever forgive me, and I'm no' askin' ye to. I dinna care what happens to me, but just please dinna let Alana and my other children or my grandchildren suffer because of the bad choices I've made in life. They are innocent and dinna deserve to live in fear and solitude because of me."

"What do ye mean? What are ye sayin'?"

Ethan felt like he was finally going to get his answers when he heard a bloodcurdling woman's scream from outside the open window. He ran over and saw a flash of white as something . . . or someone fell to the ground from the tower window.

"What was that?" Ethan's heart sped up. He knew what it was. It was the ghost of the bride of Mad Murdock.

"That? Oh, that," said Gil. "It's just the ghost of the late laird's wife of the castle."

"Mad Murdock," said Ethan under his breath.

"Aye. He killed her by pushin' her from the tower to her death."

"Then it's true!" Ethan felt very uncomfortable. His memories of his childhood when he snuck into this castle and was frightened out of his mind rose to the surface. "How often does this happen?" he asked, feeling very unsettled. "And how can ye stay here with . . . with that? Doesna it bother ye?" He didn't understand why Gil didn't even seem upset.

"It happens a lot," he said. "I dinna like it, of course no'. There are some frightenin' things that happen here, usually at night. But it keeps people away and that's why I'm here. After all, ye ken more than anyone that I am a fugitive now. What am I supposed to do?"

"Turn yerself in," spat Ethan. "Or perhaps I should do that for ye?"

"If ye do, ye'll be condemnin' Alana and the others to a life behind bars for helpin' me. Do ye really want that to happen to the girl who was once yer betrothed?"

Before he could answer, the door to the room burst open and the two guards rushed in with their swords drawn.

Immediately, Ethan drew his sword as well.

"We warned ye to leave," snarled Graeme. "Now, I guess we will be forced to take measures into our own hands."

"What's goin' on here?" asked Kirstine, pushing into the room with Finn right behind her. She looked tired and seemed out of breath as she rested her hand on her large belly.

Caleb ran up next, chewing on something while Trapper rushed into the room almost knocking over the men. "I thought I heard someone scream. Is everyone all right?" The dog turned and growled at the guards, showing its teeth.

"We warned him to go and instead we find him in here," said Albert.

"Leave him be," Gil answered from the bed. "He means us no harm."

"I dinna believe it." Graeme took a step forward while Caleb drew his sword from behind him. The guards turned, grasping their weapons, keeping an eye on both Ethan and Caleb.

"Move aside. Let me in," demanded Alana as she pushed through the men. She stopped in front of Ethan with a look of horror on her face. "Ethan! What are ye doin' in here?"

"It seems I've found yer faither," he answered.

ALANA FELT like things were going from bad to worse. The last thing she wanted was for Ethan to find her father when Diarmad had him chained to the bed. How was she going to explain this?

"He's ill," she blurted out, her eyes darting over to her father, and then back to Ethan. "He should be restin'. Ye need to leave anon."

"Alana, someone better explain to me what is goin' on around here, and they'd better do it fast," warned Ethan.

"My faither has . . . gone mad," she said, seeing the disappointment in her father's eyes by talking about him as if he'd lost his mind. Still, she had to say something to satisfy Ethan so he would hopefully leave the isle. "We've been here for years in hidin', hopin' my faither's mind would return to normal, but it hasna," she said, wishing Ethan would believe it. "He's only chained to the bed because we dinna want him to hurt himself."

"He's chained to the bed?" Ethan's brows arched in surprise.

"Losh me, Alana!" said her father. "Did ye really have to say that?" He threw his hands up in the air, pushing the blanket to the side, no longer trying to conceal his shackle.

Alana could have kicked herself when she realized Ethan hadn't known. Her father shook his head in disgust and lay back on the bed.

"Alana, I never thought ye'd be so cold as to chain up yer own faither," gasped Ethan. "Why didna ye seek out help for him? Or at least tell someone ye were here all this time?"

"Ethan, please," she begged, not wanting to have to lie to him anymore. "It would be better if ye just left the isle and never returned."

The look he gave her said it all. Hurt showed in his eyes as well as irritation. She hadn't meant for it to sound crass but he was upsetting everyone and he needed to leave. For now.

"I had Finn load the box of Osla's things onto yer boat," said Kirstine, stepping between the guards and Ethan.

"I see," said Ethan, still standing with his sword drawn.

"God's eyes, can everyone put down the weapons?" asked Alana.

"It seems to me yer laird wouldna want to harbor a thief who is goin' mad. So why is he?" asked Ethan suspiciously.

"Men, lower yer weapons," commanded Gil from the bed.

"Do it," added Alana.

The guards slowly sheathed their weapons. Ethan and Caleb did the same.

"Ethan, please. Just leave here and dinna ask anymore questions," begged Alana. "Leave this isle quickly and never return."

"Do ye really mean that?" he asked. She felt his pain like a knife driving into her heart. "After all we had together, ye are sayin' ye never want to see me again?"

"That's right," she answered, biting her bottom lip. If he didn't leave soon, she was going to start crying, and she didn't want to look weak in front of anyone right now.

"Well then. I suppose it's time for us to leave, Caleb," said Ethan.

"Aye, I suppose so." Caleb reached down and picked up his pine marten that had followed him into the room.

"Guidbye, Alana," Ethan said softly, making her want to run and throw herself into his arms, begging him never to go. She'd played the ghost again, hoping to scare him off. But now she was frightened that she would never see Ethan again. What had she done?

"Ethan, let me walk ye down to the boat," said Alana, wanting to spend a few more minutes with him. She took a step forward but he stopped her.

"Nay!" He held up a halting hand to keep her from going with him. "I'd really rather ye didna do that. Come, Trapper," he said, hurrying from the room, making Alana feel as if she'd just lost her one chance to make things right and be happy again.

* * *

As soon as Ethan and Caleb left the room, Alana pushed Albert and Graeme out of the way and headed for the door. "Why did ye have to draw yer swords on Ethan?" she spat, feeling like she'd never see him again, and that truly bothered her.

"Diarmad's ship entered the cove," announced Gil from the bed.

"That's right. We came here to do what we could to get rid of Ethan before Diarmad saw him. But how did ye ken Diarmad had returned?" Albert asked Gil.

"I saw Ethan's expression as he looked out the window," explained Alana's father.

"So . . . he saw the ship, too?" asked Alana. This was not good at all.

"I canna be sure, but I think so." The chain on Gil's leg jangled as he moved. "Ethan threatened to turn me in for what I've done."

"Do ye think he'll say anythin' when he gets back to the mainland?" asked Graeme.

"Part of me hopes he does," Alana told them. "We canna go on livin' this way."

"What are ye complainin' about now?" asked Diarmad, walking into the room with a few of his men at his heels.

"My daughter is just concerned for my health," answered Alana's father, coming to the rescue. If Diarmad didn't say anything about Ethan, then Ethan must have left without being seen. She breathed a silent sigh of relief. He was safe.

"There's nothin' wrong with yer health," grunted Diarmad. "All right, everyone down to the cove. Augey, unchain the auld man and bring him along, too. We'll need him as well as the girl to deal with these smugglers since they speak French, and we dinna."

"There are more smugglers here? Already?" asked Alana in shock. "But ye just returned from deliverin' a shipment."

"That's right. And if ye werena all up here instead of

watchin' for our ship like ye're supposed to, ye would have kent that. Now, hurry up."

"Nay," Alana answered boldly. "I refuse to help ye anymore."

"Ye willna refuse me, because if ye do, yer siblin's or mayhap that little girl of yers will suffer the consequences," growled Diarmad. "Now, let's go." He grabbed Alana by the arm so tightly that she almost screamed out loud.

"Alana will help ye," said her father from the bed. "So will I. Now get this damned chain off of my leg and leave my daughter alone."

"Kirstine, stay with Isobel," said Alana as Diarmad hauled her away. She grabbed a cloak from a hook on the wall while Augey unchained her father. She didn't like the fact that they'd been chaining him up while they were gone. She also didn't like the fact that they'd had more and more smugglers showing up in the cove lately. This life of living hell was going to have to end, and she was the only one who could do anything to stop it. Alana already missed Ethan, and felt like she'd made the wrong choice in not telling him everything while she'd had the chance. In trying to protect the others, she severed any thread of hope of ever getting back together with him. She hated herself more now than when she'd first left him at the altar.

They headed to the hidden cove, trudging through the snow. The sun was out overhead, but the cold settled in her bones, making her feel weary. She was tired of living in fear and ready to do something to change it. But to her dismay, she realized that she might have made some wrong choices concerning Ethan's visit. And because of her mistake, it might be too late to do anything about it.

CHAPTER 8

*E*than felt terrible just leaving Alana on the isle, but she had told him she wanted him to leave and she never wanted him to return. There was only so much rejection a man could take from one woman.

"I'm surprised ye and Alana didna get back together," said Caleb as they sailed the small boat to the MacKeefe shores. Caleb's pine marten lay curled up in Caleb's pouch while Ethan's dog sat in the boat whimpering, looking at the box of things that were supposedly Osla's. The dog's tail swiped back and forth over the floor of the boat.

"It's obvious that she really doesna want me," he answered, still not wanting to believe it was true.

"Are ye sure?" asked Caleb, taking a swallow of wine from a bottle that Alana had sent with them. "She still looked at ye in that same way that she used to when ye were engaged to be married, if ye didna notice."

"I think it's just yer imagination, Caleb." Ethan answered, looked out over the water and wishing it was so. The kiss they'd shared felt real. Or so she made it seem. All it did was stir feelings within him of wanting her back in his arms . . . back in his bed. "What we had was in the past and long gone. I can see now that it was all a lie."

"Is that really what ye believe?"

Ethan thought about it for a moment and let out a deep sigh. "I'm no' sure. Mayhap I'm all wrong, but it is so hard to tell. Somethin' is no' right there. I dinna understand it, but Alana is lyin' to me, I ken she is."

"Oh, ye mean about her faither? Or about the ghost?"

"About everythin'. Caleb, she just wasna herself. She seemed so cold and . . . worried."

"Time changes everyone, Ethan. Even ye."

"Aye, I suppose so. I guess I just need to let it go."

When they got to the shore, Hawke and Logan were there to greet them.

"We wondered what happened to ye," said Hawke. His bird cried out from the sky, making lazy circles in the air above them.

"We were just gettin' ready to come lookin' for ye two," added Logan. His wolf, Jack, watched them from atop a rock.

"We only stayed overnight because of the storm," said Caleb, jumping over the side of the boat into the water to help pull it to shore.

"And because Caleb likes to eat," grunted Ethan.

"Ethan, Ethan! Did ye find my doll?" Sophie came running down to the water with her brother following. "Where is Annabelle? Do ye have her?" she asked anxiously.

"We did have it, but we dinna have it now," said Caleb, making Ethan want to box his friend's ears.

"Ye found her and left her on the isle?" Sophie started wailing and all the men groaned.

Trapper barked from the boat, adding to the noise and commotion.

"Home sweet home," Ethan muttered. "Get out of the boat, Trapper," commanded Ethan, but the dog stayed there barking at the covered box of things they'd brought back for the children.

"What's that?" Oliver pointed at the box.

"Those are some of yer mathair's things," said Ethan. "Kirstine and Alana thought ye might want them."

Trapper whined and wagged his tail as Oliver jumped into the boat to eagerly look in the large box. Sophie, on the other hand, continued to cry.

"Losh me!" cried Oliver, jumping back in surprise. He knocked into Trapper and both he and the dog fell over the side of the boat and into the water.

"What are ye doin', lad?" called out Hawke, rushing over to the boat as the rest of the men laughed.

"Look," said Oliver, standing up in the water and pointing toward the box.

"Uh, Ethan," said Hawke in a solemn voice. "Ye might want to come over here and see this for yerself."

"What for?" asked Ethan. "If my hound falls in the water then he deserves to be cold and wet. He can dry off by the fire with the boy. They need to be more careful."

"Just get over here. Now," said Hawke, sounding as if it were something important.

"Sophie, come here," said Logan, picking up the crying girl. All the men walked down to the boat to see what Hawke wanted.

"All right, I'm here. What is it?" asked Ethan impatiently, eager to get to camp and out of the cold weather.

"Take that box out of the boat," said Hawke, his eyes still fastened to it.

"Egads, is that all? Couldna Oliver have taken it? I'm sure it's no' that heavy." Ethan reached over the side of the boat for the box, jumping back in surprise as something moved inside. "God's eyes, nay," he ground out. "It canna be!"

"What is it?" asked Caleb, holding his pine marten and petting it. "Did a rat get into the box?"

"I guess ye could say that," said Ethan, flipping the blanket off the top of the box. "A big rat."

When he pulled the blanket away, Isobel sat up with the doll clutched to her chest.

Sophie immediately stopped crying. "Isobel! And Annabelle!" she cried out. "Put me down, Logan. Put me down, I want to play with Isobel."

"All right, but wait until Ethan brings her to shore," instructed Logan. "We dinna want all of ye endin' up in the water."

Ethan picked up Isobel, holding her tightly as he carried her through the water to the shore. She was cold and shaking and not even wearing a cloak. "What are ye doin' on my boat?" he growled. "Yer mathair is goin' to have my head."

"I wanted to play with Sophie," said the girl. "And Annabelle was afraid and wanted to get away from that scary man."

Ethan didn't know what the little girl was talking about and, right now, neither did he care. Now he had one more problem on his hands. What was he supposed to do with Alana's daughter?

"Annabelle," said Sophie, running over, holding out her arms. Isobel handed the doll to her. Sophie smiled for the first time ever, hugging the doll to her chest. "I'm glad ye came, Isobel. And I'm glad ye protected Annabelle."

"Well, I'm no' glad about this," said Ethan. "Now I have to go back to the isle, and I had hoped to never have to return there again. Especially since I'm no' welcome."

"Well, it's goin' to have to wait," said Hawke, looking up at the sky. "I think we're in for a storm worse than the last one."

This time, thunder rumbled loudly and lightning slashed a jagged streak across the darkening sky.

"I'd suggest we all head back to camp quickly or we're goin' to get wet," said Logan. "Come on, Sophie." He scooped the girl up in one arm.

"Take Isobel, too," said Ethan, handing the girl over to him. "I'll help the others secure the boat."

This time, Isobel started wailing. "I want ye to take me, Ethan." She cried and clung to Ethan's neck.

"Go on," Hawke said from the shore. "Take Oliver with ye so he can dry off. Caleb and I will secure the boat and bring the box back to camp."

Trapper barked and ran up the shore, shaking and getting the girls wet, making them both scream.

"Let's go, lassies," Ethan told the girls. "And someone find me some wool."

"What for?" asked Logan, speaking loudly to be heard over the sound of more crying.

"To plug my ears. I dinna ken how much more of this I can take."

As soon as Alana got back to the castle, she headed straight to the fire in the great hall to get warm. It was a nasty, cold day out there. Things just got worse when the head smuggler, Rock, and his smuggling friends decided to bed down at Blackbriar. She didn't want them here. It was bad enough having Diarmad and his smuggler friends who lived here. Alana was starting to really hate her life.

After seeing Ethan again and being held in his arms, it brought to life all those feelings she had for him that she'd tried to suppress these past five years. Her heart ached for him. All she could think about since she saw him was kissing him once again.

This was no way to raise her daughter. She needed to do something about it soon. It ate away at her every day that she couldn't give her daughter a better life. It made her feel like a bad mother. Especially when she'd never even allowed little Isobel to play with Sophie when she lived on the isle. It wasn't her choice, but she'd had to do it. Diarmad and his men were always watching them, making sure they said nothing about his operation to anyone.

Diarmad. That made her think about her poor sister, Kirstine, and how she was once again carrying the cur's baby. She couldn't even imagine how awful it was for her sister to have to lay with the man and be his wife.

Alana and her siblings hadn't even left the isle since they'd moved here. She longed to see other people, have friends . . . have a life again.

The smugglers moved into the great hall making themselves at home. Alana was so cold her body trembled. Or mayhap it trembled because sending Ethan away and pretending she didn't care about him were the hardest things she'd had to do since leaving him at the altar.

As she held her hands out over the fire to warm herself, thunder rumbled the walls and rain pelted down outside. From the corners of her eyes, she saw Kirstine rushing toward her with Finn following on her heels.

"Alana," cried Kirstine, hurrying to her side. "Alana, I'm so sorry."

"It's no' yer fault these wretched thieves decided to stay the night," said Alana, still shivering. "But I dinna want them anywhere near Isobel. We need to keep her safe."

Suddenly, Alana realized that Isobel was not with her sister.

"Kirstine, where is Isobel?" she asked cautiously, not wanting to hear any further bad news. "Is she sleepin' in our chamber? Ye really shouldna have left her there alone. Ye ken how frightened she's been lately of some imaginary ghost or monster she says she saw"

"Nay, she's no' there," said Kirstine, wringing her hands in worry. Her face became pale and she swayed back and forth. "I'm sorry," she said again, making Alana's gut twist.

"Somethin' is wrong. What is it? Where is my daughter?"

Kirstine and Finn exchanged glances but didn't say a word.

"For the love of God, Sister, please dinna tell me that somethin' has happened to Isobel." Fear coursed through Alana like never before.

"Nay, I'm sure she's fine," said Kirstine. "But she is no' here in the castle."

Thunder boomed overhead and lightning flashed across the arrow slit windows.

"God's bones, dinna tell me she is out there in the storm?" Alana gripped Kirstine's arm tightly for strength, hoping she wouldn't fall over because she was so worried.

"I'm sure she's safe and warm in the MacKeefe camp by now," said Finn. "Dinna worry about her. Ethan will protect her."

"What did ye say?" asked Alana through gritted teeth. "Bid the devil, dinna tell me that Ethan kidnapped her."

"Nay, he didna even ken she was there," said Kirstine.

"That's right," agreed Finn. "She hid away on Ethan's boat."

"Ye ken this for a fact?" Alana drilled the boy.

"Aye." He nodded his head, causing a wet, blond lock of hair to fall across his face. With one swipe of his hand he pushed it away. "I helped her hide there," he said, sounding proud of it.

"Ye did what!" Alana's voice was louder than it should be and some of the men started looking their way.

"Keep yer voice down," said Kirstine. "If Diarmad finds out about this he'll string us up."

"Finn, why in heaven's name would ye do such a thing?" scolded Alana.

"She wanted to go," said the boy. "She said Annabelle wasna safe here. She thought someone was followin' her and tryin' to steal Annabelle from her."

"Annabelle is a doitit doll! Why did ye let her do such a foolish thing?"

"I dinna ken," said Finn, shrugging his shoulders. "I guess it's because I felt sorry for her. She's never had a friend except for Sophie when she used to sneak out of the castle and play with her."

"I canna believe what I'm hearin'." Alana wondered how she had never known about this when it was happening.

"I made sure ye didna ken," said Finn with a smile. "I

always went with her since Sophie's brother, Oliver, was my friend."

"Finn, I had no idea," said Alana, really feeling like a bad mother now. She'd been so concerned with her father and the smuggling that she hadn't paid close enough attention to realize where her daughter was at all times.

"I didna ken either," said Kirstine. "But Alana, ye canna blame them. What kind of life is it growin' up in this prison of a castle, trapped on this horrid isle?"

"Ye're right," said Alana, releasing a deep breath. "But I didna even think Isobel liked Ethan and would want to go with him."

"Isobel likes him," said Finn. "She just didna like that he wanted to take her doll away. But when she heard that Sophie had been cryin' for the doll, she wanted to comfort her friend. That is why she decided to go to Sophie and take her the doll herself."

"That girl is far beyond her years, I swear," said Alana shaking her head.

"What are we goin' to do?" asked Kirstine.

"I think she's safe," said Finn with a nod.

"Aye, I'm sure Ethan will take guid care of her," agreed Kirstine.

"I hope so," said Alana, pulling Kirstine and Finn to the side so the men wouldn't hear her. "I wish we could all go to the MacKeefe camp."

"Let's do it," Finn whispered back.

"Nay. We'd never be able to sneak away without Diarmad noticin'," said Alana. "Besides, I dinna want Ethan and the MacKeefes involved in any of this. Those smugglers would try to slit their throats if they came anywhere near here."

"We've got to do somethin' about Isobel," said Kirstine.

"True. If Diarmad and the others ken she is with the MacKeefes, it'll mean trouble for all of us. Thankfully, the castle is filled with smugglers now and that will take Diarmad's attention."

"What do ye mean?" asked Finn.

"What she means is that Isobel kens too much about the smugglin' ring," said Kirstine.

"She's young. I'm sure she doesna even understand what goes on here," protested Finn.

"Mayhap no', but Diarmad willna care," said Alana, watching the man from across the room. "He willna want to take the chance that he will be discovered."

"Then we canna let him ken that she is gone," said Kirstine.

"Nay. If so, he'll do somethin' horrible to us or mayhap to Faither."

"I'm frightened," said Finn, looking like he was about to cry.

"Things will be better soon, I promise," said Alana, pulling the two of them to her in a hug. "Now, make up a story that I went to sleep early because I am ill and that Isobel is in bed, too. Kirstine and Finn, ye both can speak French, so help Faither communicate with thee smugglers. Whatever ye do, just keep Diarmad away from my chamber."

"I think I can keep Diarmad occupied," said Kirstine. "But what are ye goin' to do?"

"I'm goin' to use the small boat Finn has constructed and hid in the reeds on the bank. I'm goin' to sail tonight to the MacKeefe camp."

"In the storm?" Kirstine was horrified. "Nay, Sister, it is too dangerous. Please dinna go."

"My daughter is missin'. Nothin' is too dangerous as far as I'm concerned. I need to get her back."

"I understand," said Kirstine, putting both hands on her belly. "If I ever have a bairn that survives, I am sure I'll feel the same way, too."

"Ye will have a healthy bairn and it will be soon," said Alana, putting her hand on her sister's belly and feeling the baby kick. They both laughed.

"Are ye goin' to ask the MacKeefes to help us?" Finn asked, looking ever so hopeful.

"Nay," she said, wishing it were the case. "I'm goin' there to get Isobel and bring her back and that is all. I dinna want their clan involved."

"I hope ye can make it across the water to the mainland," said Kirstine. "There is a nasty squall brewin' out there."

"It's the chance I'll have to take," said Alana, heading for the door. She was afraid of Diarmad and the smugglers, but that's not what worried her the most. The part that made her terrified was the fact she was going to see Ethan again. And this time, she was going before the entire MacKeefe Clan. She didn't think for one minute she'd be welcome there after leaving Ethan stranded on their wedding day. To them, she would be considered naught but a strumpet or a traitor. And the worst part was that she was starting to feel like that was exactly who she was.

CHAPTER 9

"Hold me," said little Isobel to Ethan as he sat around the fire inside one of the MacKeefe buildings, wondering what the hell he was going to do with the girl.

"What?" he mumbled, taking a drink of his Mountain Magic, not really listening to her since his worried thoughts filled his head.

"I miss my mathair," she said. "Can I sit on yer lap?"

Ethan looked up to see his friends, Hawke, Caleb and Logan, all staring at him. They sat or stood far from him, looking like they were afraid to come closer.

"Well? Ye heard the girl." Hawke looked up and chuckled. That is, until little Sophie crawled atop his lap, clinging to her doll.

"I want to sit on yer lap, Hawke," said the little girl.

Logan and Caleb burst out laughing at Hawke's expression.

"Och, why no'?" he said, putting one arm around Sophie.

"My turn," said Isobel, climbing up on Ethan's lap before he had a chance to object.

"So this girl was a stowaway from the haunted castle?" asked Bridget, probably already devising a story in her head to scribble into the Highland Chronicles. She always seemed to be around when Ethan needed to talk to his friends. He had to watch what he said around her. She'd tell her father and it might end up in that book, and that wouldn't be good for Alana. It could bring trouble to her and her family if too many people knew where they were.

"Caleb," said Ethan, trying to give his friend an inconspicuous nod of his head to take the woman somewhere else. After all, Caleb fancied her, even though Ethan couldn't understand why.

"Huh?" asked Caleb, eating again as always. For such a small man, he seemed to eat twice as much as the others.

"Dinna ye want to show Bridget somethin'?"

"What?" asked Caleb, licking off his fingers.

"Tell me more about the isle and the castle," said the girl, pushing her way closer, leaning forward so she wouldn't miss a word. "Whose child is this? And does someone actually live in those ruins?"

Ethan groaned. "Caleb, mayhap ye'd like to get Bridget a drink?"

"Nay, I'm fine," she said, looking down at little Isobel. "What is her name?"

"It's Isobel," he mumbled as the little girl's eyes closed and she snuggled up contentedly against his chest to sleep.

"She looks a lot like ye," said Bridget.

His head snapped up at that comment. "Nay she doesna," he said, perusing the girl. Then he decided mayhap she did look like him a little, but it was only a coincidence, naught else.

"Aye, she does. She's got those big, round, brown eyes like yers and her hair is the same color as yers," continued Bridget.

"A lot of children do. It's common," he said, once again looking over at Caleb who was just about to take a big bite of a cinnamon custard tart.

Logan understood, and snatched the tart away from Caleb, shoving the whole thing in his mouth at once.

"Losh me! What did ye do that for?" Caleb jumped to his feet, looking like he was ready to punch Logan.

"Mayhap ye'd better get another one," said Hawke.

"And take Bridget with ye," added Ethan.

Finally, Caleb caught on. "Oh, aye. Bridget, why dinna we go find a tart or two?"

His friends burst out laughing.

Caleb took her by the arm. "I mean food . . . no' the other kind of tart," he said, sounding embarrassed.

"But I wanted to ask Ethan more about the isle," Bridget protested. "Then again, ye were there, too, so mayhap ye can tell me about it instead." She smiled but Caleb threw his friends a look that said he needed saving as they headed away.

Ethan looked down at the little girl in his arms, not able to think of anything else except that she was Alana's child. That made him wonder about the girl's father. His heart ached, thinking of what Bridget said, that she looked like him. If he and Alana had married, would their child have looked like this? He wondered.

Holding Isobel tightly in his arms, he felt like he wanted to protect her. Even if this wee lass wasn't his own, he still felt that by holding her, he was closer to Alana in some way.

"She looks guid in yer arms," said Hawke, bringing Ethan from his thoughts.

"Same to ye," said Ethan, smiling since Hawke was in a similar situation as he.

"Och, ye two are actin' like auld married men." Logan waved his hand through the air in disgust. "Come on, Jack, let's go hunt down a fox or a lassie or something that is more excitin' than sittin' here watchin' this!" He and his wolf left.

Hawke's wife, Phoebe, walked up next with their laird, Storm, and his wife, Wren.

"I think it's time for Sophie to go to sleep," said Phoebe, reaching out and taking the child from Hawke.

"I'll take Isobel," Wren offered, lifting her from Ethan's arms. After they left, Storm cleared his throat, sitting down on a bench.

"Did ye want to talk about this?" asked Storm.

"No' really." Ethan would have to explain things to the clan's chieftain now, and that was not going to be enjoyable. He sighed and started to talk. "The wee lass is Alana's daughter," he explained. "I found Alana livin' in Blackbriar Castle."

"Alana?" Storm frowned.

"Chisholm," Hawke told his father. "Ye remember the lass Ethan was goin' to marry five years ago."

"Aye," said Storm, raising his brows. "So she disappeared after leavin' ye at the altar just to live in a haunted castle on a deserted isle?"

"It seems so," Ethan answered, looking at the floor.

"What's goin' on?" asked Storm in a low voice.

"I wish I kent the answer to that," Ethan answered. "Somethin' was odd there. It just wasna right."

"Ye mean, with the ghost and all?" asked Hawke with a

smile.

"Nay, no' just the ghost, although that was unsettlin', too. It seems no one cared about the ghost or was even frightened by it."

"Except for ye," chuckled Hawke, getting a stern look from his father.

"Ye ken ye canna keep the child here," said Storm. "It's no' right and will only cause trouble. Ye need to take her back to her mathair."

"I ken. I will do it first thing in the mornin'." Ethan stood, wanting more than anything to get some sleep and to think things over. "There was somethin' else that really bothered me," he said.

"What's that?" Storm stood and so did Hawke.

"She said her faither was goin' mad. They kept him chained up in his room because of it."

"What's odd about that?" asked Hawke. "I'd have him chained up, too, if I were in their position."

"Was he a prisoner?" asked Storm, mimicking Ethan's thoughts exactly.

"I think so. He must be there against his will because I doubt that Alana would do somethin' like that to her faither even if he was goin' mad."

"What about the rest of her family? Were they there as well?" asked Hawke.

"Only her pregnant sister, Kirstine, and her brother, Finn. Her mathair is dead."

"Well, mayhap we should check it out," said Storm. "We are the closest clan to the isle."

"Nay." Ethan shook his head. "Alana doesna want me there."

"Where was the faither of her baby?" asked Storm. "Who is he?"

"I believe he's dead, and I have no idea who he was. I didna ask and I am no' sure I really ever want to ken. Excuse me now, because I need some rest."

Ethan left the building, heading to a small hut that he shared with his friends. It was still storming and raining relentlessly, but Ethan felt numb because of what happened. He didn't seem to notice the weather. He was about to go inside when he thought he saw movement from down where the boat was docked. If a thief in the night were trying to steal it, he'd give them a little surprise.

Unsheathing his sword, he hurried down to the water, so upset and angry after being at the castle that whatever poor soul was there trying to steal his boat was going to end up missing a hand or perhaps his head.

FRIGID, slushy rain sliced down on Alana as she rowed the small boat to the mainland shore in the choppy water. The storm was too much for the small boat. But once she started out, it was too late to turn back. It had a small sail on it that she'd used to make it halfway across. But the wind was relentless, blowing her off course, so she'd taken the sail down and opted to row instead.

Her muscles ached and she could barely feel her fingers and toes anymore because she was too cold. She wore a cloak with a hood but it did little to keep her dry. If she didn't want to die before, she surely did now. Then again, the storm might make that decision for her.

Pushing her fears aside, she decided she didn't care how cold she was or what she had to do to get there, it no longer mattered. All she cared about was making sure her baby was safe. Why couldn't she spend more time with her child instead of attending to things that didn't matter to her? If she died in this storm before she made it to shore, she'd never see Isobel again. Her heart ached to even think this way, and she decided to focus on the shoreline and row faster.

The last place she really wanted to be right now was the MacKeefe camp, but she didn't have a choice. Isobel made that decision for her. Alana hadn't been here since the day she'd almost married Ethan and become not only his wife but also a part of the clan. Every single one of the MacKeefes had been friendly and kind to her, and now she regretted having to see them again but on totally different terms.

Because of leaving him with no explanation, she was sure his clan would not take kindly to her and neither could she blame them. If she were in Ethan's position, she would be sure to hate her, too.

Her long cloak dragged behind her as she jumped from the boat in ankle-high water and pulled the boat to the shore. Her body was so cold that she couldn't bend her fingers. She felt like a block of ice. But at least she was alive, and had made it here to bring Isobel back with her. She noticed the boat that Ethan had used, tied up next to her. She wrapped a line from her boat around the same stake he'd used since there were no trees this close to the water.

She'd just finished tying the knot when someone jumped out from behind a large rock in the dark, about scaring her out of her mind.

"Who goes there?" came a deep, gruff voice.

Her body stiffened.

As the man emerged, she saw the shine of his sword glimmering in the scarce moonlight.

"It's me! Alana," she cried. "Please dinna hurt me. I mean no harm."

"Alana?" The sword slowly lowered and the man walked forward, allowing her to see that it was Ethan.

"Ethan!" she exclaimed. Her heartbeat sped up now.

"What are ye doin' sneakin' around in the dark? I thought ye were a thief stealin' the boat. I almost took yer head off."

"I'm sorry," she said, wrapping her arms around her wet cloak, her teeth chattering. "I found out Isobel hid away on yer boat and I've come to get her and take her back to the castle."

A flash of lightning lit up the sky, hitting a tree nearby. The boom of thunder and the sound of splintering wood filled the air, making her jump.

Immediately, Ethan was there, pulling her into his arms and against him in a protective hold. "Let's get the hell out of here, Lanny," he said, using the terms of endearment he used to call her years ago. That is, when they were lovers.

Together, with his arm around her shoulders, they ran back to the camp in the rain. He brought her into the main longhouse causing everyone to look up in surprise.

"Ethan?" asked Logan with a chuckle. "Where did ye find her?"

"I'm here for my daughter," said Alana, feeling uncomfortable under the perusal of so many MacKeefes.

"Wasna she the one who escaped Ethan before they were married?" a teenaged boy asked his mother.

"No' escaped," his mother corrected him. "She left him

standin' alone like a stray dog at the altar while she went off with another man."

"Ye are no' welcome here," shouted a man from the back of the room.

"She's a strumpet," said someone else.

"Enough!" shouted Storm, getting up and holding up a hand for silence. "We are MacKeefes. We dinna treat guests with such disrespect."

"She's no guest," mumbled someone else.

"Alana Chisholm. Welcome," said Storm's wife, Lady Wren, hurrying across the room to greet her.

Alana remembered Lady Wren and had always thought she was one of the kindest people she'd ever met. She was English, yet the clan had accepted her. Alana hoped that mayhap they would all forgive her in time for what she had done to Ethan.

"Lady Wren, I've come for my daughter, Isobel," explained Alana. "It seems she hid away on Ethan's boat. I'm sorry."

"Your daughter is safe," Wren assured her. "And you are soaked to the skin. Let me get you something dry to wear and a bite to eat. You can warm yourself by the fire."

"Nay, but thank ye," she said, feeling too nervous around Ethan and not wanting to stay where she wasn't wanted. Besides, she needed to get back to the castle before she was discovered missing. "I'll just take my daughter and go."

"Yer daughter is sleepin'," said Hawke's wife, Phoebe, walking up to join them. "We just put the lassies to bed. Ye must stay for now. Ye canna take the wee one out in this storm."

"That's right," agreed Ethan. "It's too dangerous. And ye are wet and shiverin'. Ye should stay here for the night and wait out the storm."

My, how the tables had turned, thought Alana. She was the one who insisted Ethan stay at Blackbriar Castle when he wanted to leave. Now she was in the same situation.

"I really do need to get back," she protested.

"Why?" asked Ethan. "Ye seem afraid of somethin'. Is yer laird, Diarmad, goin' to give ye trouble? Because if so, I'll be sure to set him straight."

"Nay," she said, her heart beating wildly. She wasn't sure at this point if Ethan and his friends were going to storm Blackbriar or if perhaps Diarmad and her father would show up here in MacKeefe territory instead. Either one would be unfortunate. "I – I suppose I could use a bite to eat and to warm myself at the fire."

"Ye'll stay the night," insisted Ethan. "I willna let ye and the wee lass go out on the water in a storm at night. It is much too dangerous."

Alana's eyes darted around the room. Everyone was quiet and watching her. She'd never felt so uneasy in her life. "All right, if ye insist," she finally agreed.

"Good," said Lady Wren with a smile. "Phoebe, get Alana something dry to wear. She can stay in the hospice overnight where the guests sleep."

"Is my daughter there?" asked Alana, longing to see little Isobel to make sure she was safe.

"Nay, she's sleepin' in our hut," said Phoebe. "She wanted to be by her friend, Sophie, who is now my and Hawke's daughter."

"I see," said Alana, still feeling uncomfortable.

"I can take ye to see her if ye'd like," offered Ethan. "But first, ye need to get dry and warm."

"All right. I would like that," said Alana, looking up into

Ethan's caring eyes. "Ye are soaked from the rain as well," she said, reaching out to touch his wet leine.

"I will no' melt," he assured her and flashed a quick smile. Alana liked seeing Ethan smiling again. It gave her hope that she hadn't ruined the man's life after all and that, mayhap, he could still be happy someday.

"Ethan said ye are livin' at that haunted castle," remarked Storm, sounding suspicious. "Why?"

"Why?" she asked, suddenly becoming very nervous again. "It is my home now," she said.

"Where have ye been for the last five years?" asked Storm. "And why didna ye tell Ethan where ye were?"

"Aye," said Hawke, joining in with his father's investigative questions. "And why did ye leave him on yer weddin' day to begin with?"

"I – I –" she looked up at Ethan, seeing the sadness in his eyes. "It's a long story," she said, touching her cheek that felt frozen and like it was on fire all at the same time. "I'm feelin' lightheaded and I'd hate to swoon. I think I need to sit down."

"Of course, dear," said Wren, giving her husband and son a nasty glare. "What is the matter with ye two? Alana has gone through a lot to get here and I'm sure she is worried sick about her daughter."

"That's right," added Phoebe, coming to her aid. "Let her rest. I'm sure she'll answer everyone's questions in the mornin'."

"Aye. In the mornin'," agreed Alana, knowing now that she had to find Isobel and sneak her out of the MacKeefe camp and go back to the castle before dawn. If not, she was going to have to answer questions that she couldn't. Suddenly, coming here didn't seem like such a good idea after all.

CHAPTER 10

*T*rapper followed right on Ethan's heels later that night as he burst into the bunkhouse he shared with Logan and Caleb.

"Out!" commanded Ethan, causing his friends to look up. Caleb was already lying in bed with his pine marten snuggled up on his chest. Logan sat at the fire polishing his sword while his wolf lay curled up on a blanket in the corner of the one-room house.

"What?" Caleb sat up halfway in bed, holding on to his pet.

"What's this all about?" grumbled Logan, slowly lowering his sword.

"I'm goin' to need some privacy with Alana," Ethan answered.

"Och, is that all?" Caleb laid back down. "Go ahead and bed her, we willna bother ye."

"Aye, we can even hang a blanket up over there." Logan pointed with the tip of his sword. "Now that Hawke's no longer sharin' the place with us, ye two will have plenty of room to . . . do yer thing."

"I never said I wanted to bed her," replied Ethan, not that the idea hadn't crossed his mind. "I havena been alone with her since she . . . since she . . ."

"Dumped ye," said Caleb, yawning and closing his eyes. "Ye still canna even say it yet, can ye?"

Logan smiled and continued to polish his sword. "Mayhap we should stay here. That way, if she tries to leave ye again, we can hold her down and keep her from runnin'."

"That's enough." Ethan walked over and took the sword from Logan's hand, laying it on the table. "Now, I mean it. I want to talk with her alone. I'll never find out what's goin' on with ye two simpkins sittin' here distractin' her." In two long strides, he was across the room, yanking the covers off of Caleb and pulling him to his feet. The pine marten hissed and ran out the open door followed by the wolf. Trapper started to follow but Ethan stopped him.

"Stay, boy," he commanded and his dog sat down, still looking anxious like it wanted to chase his friends.

"Blethers, ye left the door open and now I need to go out in the cold and find Slink," complained Caleb. He was bare-footed and wearing nothing but his braies.

"Guid idea. So go," said Ethan, swishing his hand in the air. "I told Alana to meet me here when she was done visitin' with her daughter. She will be arrivin' at any minute."

"Hello?" Alana stuck her head in the door. "Is anyone home?"

"Alana!" Caleb half-turned, holding his hands over his groin area. "Dinna look."

"Egads, Caleb, it's no' like there's anythin' to see." Ethan walked over and grabbed a cloak from the wall and a pair of boots and handed them to Caleb. "Guidbye," he said. "Dinna hurry back, ye two."

"Come on, Caleb, we'll find somethin' better to do because this looks like it's goin' to be borin'," complained Logan, grabbing his cloak and heading out the door. Caleb still stood there, not knowing what to do.

"Ye, too." Ethan took Caleb by the elbow and hauled him across the room.

"Wait! I dinna have my boots on yet." Caleb held the boots in one hand and the cloak in front of his nearly naked body with the other.

With Alana inside the building, Ethan pushed Caleb outside and slammed the door behind him. Immediately, a soft knocking noise was heard.

"I need my clothes," came Caleb's muffled voice from the other side of the door.

Ethan grabbed some clothes on a pile on the floor, knowing that is where Caleb always left his. He opened the door and his hand shot out. "Here." He dropped them in Caleb's hands.

"Thank y-" Caleb's words were cut off as Ethan slammed the door in his face. He turned around to find Alana giggling, standing, warming her hands by the fire.

"Ye're laughin'," he said softly.

"Aye. I'm sorry," she apologized. "It just struck me as funny, that's all. Yer friends are special. I promise no' to laugh again."

"Nay." He strolled across the room, his eyes focused on her. "I like it when ye giggle. It reminds me of the girl I used to ken."

She stopped giggling then and stared into the fire. As he came closer, he swore he saw tears in her eyes.

"What we had was a guid thing, Ethan. But that . . . that was a long time ago."

"What happened?" he whispered, coming up behind her. "Why did ye leave me when I thought ye loved me?"

She turned and looked up into his eyes. "I did love ye. And I still do." She seemed sincere, and this only confused him more.

"Then why in heaven's name did ye leave me on our weddin' day?"

"I canna answer that, Ethan."

"Why no'?" he growled. "Dinna ye think I deserve an answer?"

"Of course, ye do. But . . . but I canna give ye yer answer just yet."

"Then tell me this. Was it because ye were in love with another man?" Ethan's hands balled into fists as he considered the possibility.

"Nay!" she cried. "I've never loved anyone but ye, Ethan. Ye need to believe me."

"How can I?" he asked, turning his head and looking the other way. He clenched his jaw as he spoke. "I havena seen ye in five years, and ye never had the consideration to tell me ye birthed another man's baby."

"Nay, it's no' like that. Ye dinna understand."

In anger, Ethan knocked over a chair and stormed to the other side of the room. "Nay, I dinna understand, and I urge ye to explain now because I am losin' my patience."

"Dinna threaten me," she spat, and then broke down and started crying.

Ethan always had a weakness for crying lassies. Especially

ones he cared about. He didn't want to see Alana so sad, and felt now that he had made her cry.

"I'm sorry," he whispered, walking closer.

She sat down on the edge of a bed and hid her face in her hands. "Nay, I'm the one who is sorry, Ethan. I have ruined everythin' guid I've ever had in my life."

Gently, he sat on the pallet next to her and pulled her hands away from her face.

"I had hoped to marry ye and have a family with ye, Alana. We were lucky enough no' to have been betrothed just for the sake of an alliance. We fell in love. On our own. Or so I thought. That is somethin' that is rare. I felt we had somethin' special between us."

"We did, Ethan. And I hope we still can."

"How?" he asked. "I canna even get ye to be honest with me. How can I ever trust ye again?"

"I want to tell ye things, honest I do. But ye have to believe me when I say I canna."

"Why? That makes no sense." He stood up and started pacing the floor.

"Because if I do, those I love might be hurt."

He stopped pacing. "Too late for that," he said, hearing the sarcasm dripping from his own words. Still, he didn't care. It no longer mattered. "Mayhap this was a mistake bringin' ye here," he said, heading for the door. "Ye can stay here tonight and in the mornin' I'll personally take ye back to yer castle and we'll never have to see each other again."

"Nay, dinna be that way, Ethan."

He pulled open the door and was about to step out into the cold when her next words stopped him in his tracks.

ELIZABETH ROSE

"Ye wanted to ken who Isobel's faither is, so I'm goin' to tell ye."

Suddenly, Ethan felt as if he didn't really want to know. "I dinna care," he said without turning around, taking a step outside. "Mayhap some things in life are better off left unkenned."

"It's ye," she said as he was shutting the door. He froze in his tracks and slowly turned around.

"What did ye say?" he asked, thinking he'd misheard her, but hoping he had not.

"Ye are Isobel's faither." Tears streamed down her cheeks.

He stepped back into the hut and slowly closed the door. He didn't know how to react. Elation, joy, surprise . . . and also anger shot through him all at once.

"Are ye sayin' I've had a daughter for the past five years and ye couldna bother to tell me? What kind of lassie are ye?"

ALANA'S MOUTH DROPPED OPEN. For some reason, she thought Ethan would be happy to know he'd sired a child. But instead, he seemed to think she was some kind of ogre for not telling him sooner.

"I'm sorry, Ethan, but I wasna here to tell ye. I lived in Ireland up to this past year. And I was ill after birthin' Isobel for a long time. I nearly died to bring her into this world." She couldn't hold her tears back and began crying more.

"Och, I'm sorry about that," he said in a half-whisper. "I didna ken."

"I didna ken I was pregnant until right before our weddin' day. I wanted to surprise ye and tell ye after we'd said our vows, but that never happened. I – I had to leave, and so I did."

He came toward her slowly, stalking her in a way. "Ye had to leave or ye chose to leave?" he asked, putting her in an awkward position.

"I was called away the day of our weddin'. I had to go."

"To steal another herd besides the MacKeefes?"

"Nay!" she spat. "I didna ken anythin' about that, no matter if ye believe it or no'. I had to leave quickly and had no time to say guidbye. It was urgent. My family needed me."

"And what about me, Lanny? Didna ye think I might have needed ye, too? And what about Isobel? Who does she think her faither is?"

"I never told her. Since she doesna have a faither, she decided he was dead. She doesna ask questions about it."

"And does that make it right?" he challenged her.

"Nay," she said, shaking her head, feeling guilty on so many levels. "I'm a horrible person for the things I've done to ye, but I had to make a choice that day and it changed my life in ways I never expected – and they werena guid. I did the only thing I could at the time. I was told my mathair's life was in danger, my uncle had died, and my faither was runnin' for his life. I swear, I didna ken it was goin' to end up this way. I only hope someday ye will be able to forgive me."

"When ye stop lyin' to me, mayhap I will. But that is yet to be seen."

"That's the truth, Ethan. It is no' a lie. Hold me," she said, her body trembling, tears streaming down her face. "I need ye. Isobel needs ye. I am livin' a life of hell and I dinna ken how to make things right."

"Oh, Lanny," he said, reaching out and resting his hands on her shoulders. "Ye ken it is my weakness when ye cry."

"I never meant to hurt ye, Ethan. Ye've got to believe me."

He looked into her eyes and sighed. "I might be the biggest fool to walk the earth, but I do believe ye, sweetheart. I see the turmoil in yer eyes. I dinna ken what ye are goin' through but I want to help ye if I can. However, I canna do that if ye willna tell me everythin'."

"I ken," she said, knowing she should tell him more, but worried about his reaction. "I told ye that ye have a daughter, and yet ye dinna even seem to care."

"Ye're wrong," said Ethan, holding her shoulders and looking into her eyes. "I am thrilled beyond measure that yer bairn is mine and no' another man's."

"But do ye like her? Do ye think ye can learn to love Isobel someday?"

"I do. But I also want to tell ye that I never stopped lovin' ye either."

With that, he pulled her to him and kissed her passionately on the mouth. Her head fell back and her eyes closed as her body came to life under Ethan's touch. Her lips parted slightly. As the kiss deepened, his tongue shot out and entered her mouth, making her almost cry out.

This reminded her so much of the first . . . and only time they'd made love. It was the day they'd gotten betrothed. They'd been celebrating and both had a little too much Mountain Magic that night. They should have waited until the wedding to couple, but neither of them could wait. They'd made love that night and it was the best night of her life. One time was all it took to create something so wonderful between them that she could barely even believe it happened.

His hands slid down her back and rested on her rear, making her warm up quickly. As he continued to kiss her, he gave her bottom end a little squeeze and his moan of pleasure vibrated against her lips. Alana melted in his arms. She'd missed this so much over the years that she'd dreamed about it almost every night. She always felt so protected when she was in Ethan's arms. Protected, and loved.

"Lay with me, Ethan," she begged him, gently reaching up and nibbling on his ear. When he shifted slightly and she leaned in closer to him, she felt the hard bulge beneath his plaid and knew he wanted it too.

"What did ye say, lassie?" He pulled back and looked into her eyes.

"I'm sorry for everythin'," she said. "And I want ye to ken that I've never been with any other man but ye."

"Really?" he asked, seeming surprised as well as pleased.

"I've been forced to make some choices that have made both of us miserable through the years. I –"

Her words were cut off when Ethan kissed her again, picking her up into his arms. "No more talkin' tonight," he said against her lips as he carried her over to the bed and lay her down upon it. "The way I see it, we have five years of catchin' up to do."

When tears of joy slipped down her cheeks, he reached out with his thumb and wiped her tears away.

"Do ye mean it?" she asked, her breathing becoming deep as she watched the rise and fall of her own chest. The thought of making love with Ethan already had her tingling from head to toe.

"I dinna want to see ye cry, lass. I just found out I have a daughter and I'd like to spend some intimate time with her mathair if ye dinna object."

"I'd like that, Ethan," she said, feeling like she didn't deserve him, but happy that he decided he wanted her in this way after all. Mayhap she could find that happiness again that she'd known with Ethan when life was so much simpler and before her world had come crashing down around her.

"I dinna want to push, Lanny. But when ye are ready to tell me everythin', I am here to listen. I want to ken. We have a lifetime to figure out the answers to our problems . . . together," he told her, reaching out and untying the lacing on her bodice. "But right now, all of that can wait. There is somethin' else I think this is long overdue."

"I agree," she whispered as he pulled open her bodice, reaching down and pressing his mouth against her skin at the base of her neck. Her body heated under his mouth – under his touch – as he left a trail of kisses down her cleavage, getting nearer and nearer to her breasts. The anticipation already had her breasts aching to be touched. She wanted him to suckle her and lick every part of her body.

"What's this?" he asked, picking up the key she wore on a string around her neck along with their wedding ring. She had almost forgotten it was there.

"It's nothin'," she said as he perused the key in the palm of his hand.

"It looks auld. What does it open? And is that our weddin' ring? Did ye steal it, Lanny? How could ye?"

"I didna steal it. I . . . found it, down at the boat the day I left. I am no' sure how it got there."

"I was told Slink stole the ring, so mayhap that is the answer. What about the key?"

"It's just a momento from my late mathair," she said, taking it from him and slipping the string over her neck, placing the key down next to her on the bed along with the ring. "I dinna even ken what that key opens. It's no' important."

As he exposed one of her breasts, she gasped at the feel of his hand cupping her and his thumb flicking over her nipple, making it instantly taut. And when he lowered his head to her, she closed her eyes and arched her back, pulling him closer as he took her into his mouth.

He closed his lips over her nipple, suckling at her like a babe to its mother, making her moan in delight. Then he released her and flicked his tongue over her hard peak, about driving her out of her mind.

"Ye like that, lass?" he whispered in a sultry voice.

"Mmmm," she answered, breathing heavily, barely able to speak.

But as good as that felt, it was nothing compared to what he did next. He pushed up her skirt and pulled down her braies slowly, letting his hot hands run the length of her thighs, making her quiver. Tossing her undergarments to the floor, he focused his gaze on her nether regions, already triggering a wetness between her thighs.

"Lookin' at yer beauty in the firelight, it makes me feel like it's the first time again that we've ever made love."

"Let's pretend it is," she whispered back, reaching out and running her hands over his hard chest, letting her fingers slip underneath his leine.

"Och, these clothes are just gettin' in the way," he said impatiently, standing up and removing every stitch of clothing and kicking off his boots as well. Her mouth went dry when she took in the view of his hard chest and thick, corded muscles in his upper arms. Her gaze slid down his toned body, past his flat stomach and down past his waist to his dark, curly hair. His erection was bigger than she'd remembered and she wondered if he was as desperate for a good bedding as she was right now.

Her attention was diverted when Trapper whined from the corner, curling up near the fire. She'd almost forgotten that the dog was even there, nor did she care. All she could think about was being alone again with Ethan – the man she admired, adored, and loved.

"Ethan," she said, pushing up to her elbows, drinking in the enticing sight of his naked body. Her breathing labored as her eyes scanned down his body and settled below his waist once more. He was hard and ready and she'd never seen him this engorged. "Ye really do want me," she said, the thought of making love with him exciting her even more.

"We'll never do this unless ye remove some clothin' as well."

Kneeling down next to the bed, he kissed her, taking hold of her skirt in both hands. "I like how ye look wearin' the MacKeefe plaid," he told her. "It's what ye should be wearin', lass."

"Aye. I like it, too," she admitted as he slipped her tunic over her head and removed the plaid, leaving her naked.

"God, I missed ye, Lanny." He ran his hands up her torso, making her shiver with delicious anticipation of what was yet to come. Then he leaned forward and licked her stomach, making her squirm.

"Ye are drivin' me mad, Ethan MacKeefe," she said in a breathy whisper, feeling like she was going to lose control.

"Well, then ye ken how I have felt for the last five years." One hand cupped her breast while his mouth closed over the other nipple. In his sensuous way, he drew her in, as his nimble fingers played with her other peak. His thumb teased her tip again until she arched up off the bed.

"I want ye, Ethan," she whispered against his neck, kissing him and running her hands around the back of him, playfully squeezing his tight buttocks.

"Och," he mumbled, pushing his hardened form up against her womanhood. "Lanny, ye ken I like foreplay more than anyone. But in this case, it has been so long that I feel as if I am goin' to burst. If I dinna enter ye now, it's goin' to be over before it goes any further."

"There's no need to wait, Ethan. I am ready and more than willing."

That was all he needed to hear. He used his hands to spread her legs, settling himself between them, running his fingers over her womanly mound, testing her readiness by playing with her folds and slipping a finger inside her.

She gasped as she climbed higher, almost ready to shatter just under his touch. With her eyes closed and her body awakened, she could no longer wait.

"I told ye I am ready, Ethan. Please, do no' tease me any longer."

"I'd like this to last forever since it's been so long, but I willna tempt either of us further."

A moan of ecstasy left her lips as her lover slid his hardened form into her. He felt so hot, so big. She wet her lips with her tongue, breathing heavily, waiting in anticipation for what was to come next.

And when he slid his shaft in and out, guided by her liquid passion, she could no longer hold back, and cried out as she found her release.

"Ooooooh, Ethan!" she cooed, squirming beneath him,

wanting to feel every bit of his manly beauty as he took her as his lover. They did the dance of love, and she instantly forgot about all her troubles. No longer was she living in hell, because this felt like heaven.

"Aaaah," he moaned in pleasure, matching her. "This feels so guid."

And then his seed of life filled her as he was brought to the precipice of delight and took a leap over the edge.

The idea of possibly getting pregnant with another child of Ethan's was all Alana had been able to think about since Isobel was born. She pulled him to her, clinging to him, crying again, but this time because she was so happy.

"Losh me," he said through rugged breaths, pulling out and lying next to her, holding her tightly in his arms. "Ye're cryin' again. I didna please ye. It's goin' to take me a few minutes to regain my composure, but mayhap I can do somethin' else to make ye smile."

"Nay, Ethan," she said, burying her head against his chest. "I am pleased, believe me. I am only cryin' because I am so happy. In yer arms is where I feel I belong."

"Ye do belong here," he told her, kissing her atop her head. "And I've decided that ye and Isobel will stay here at the MacKeefe camp from now on."

"What?" she asked, her smile fading since she wasn't expecting him to say this – especially not right now.

"We'll tell Isobel in the mornin' that I am her faither. And then we'll get married right away."

"But – but Ethan, I need to go back to the castle," she told him, suddenly feeling very frightened again. Thoughts filled her head of Diarmad and how angry he'd be if she did not return. She pictured her pregnant sister being beaten and her brother possibly being flogged by the man. She could almost see her poor father still chained to the bed, trying to help but falling over dead since he was so ill and weak. One thought after another cascaded through her mind until all the joy and happiness she'd felt making love with Ethan had disappeared. "My siblin's and my faither are still there on the isle."

"It's all right. We'll bring them all here," he told her nonchalantly as if it would be no problem at all. "I'm sure I can convince Storm to let them stay at the MacKeefe camp for as long as they want. If yer clan willna welcome ye back, mayhap the MacKeefes can take ye in instead."

"I see," she said, realizing Ethan was living in a dream world. No clan would ever welcome her father with open arms. The MacKeefes might not be as willing as he thought to take her back either. After all, she heard the comments from them when she'd first arrived. She was sure she was not welcome, no matter what Ethan thought.

She wondered now if telling him he was a father as well as lying with him was perhaps a big mistake. If she didn't return to the isle, there would be trouble. As it was, she needed to hide the fact she was here at all. If Diarmad thought she told the MacKeefes about the smuggling ring, he was going to be furious. She wasn't sure what would happen, but it wasn't a risk she wanted to take. She had to sneak back before Diarmad even realized she and her daughter were missing. There was no other way.

Once again, Alana felt doomed, having to make a hard decision. She could no longer stay here, but she couldn't very well take her daughter away from Ethan either. Sadly, she realized that mayhap she couldn't protect her daughter after all.

There was only one thing she could do, and it was going to be even harder than leaving Ethan in the first place. She'd have to leave Isobel here in Ethan's care, and go back to the castle without her. It was the only chance she had of Ethan not coming after her and getting killed by Diarmad and his men. He would never stay put now that he knew Isobel was his daughter. But if she left the girl here, at least Ethan and the MacKeefes would keep her safe until Alana decided how she was going to fix the mess she was in. Hopefully, she could figure out a way to escape Diarmad, bring Kirstine and Finn here, and also clear her father's name. There didn't seem to be much hope, but she believed in miracles.

Alana had one chance to do this, and she had to make it work. If not, and if she failed, she was going to lose someone she loved.

All she had to do now was wait for Ethan to fall asleep, and sneak back to Blackbriar Castle to try to make things right.

CHAPTER 11

*A*lana hadn't meant to oversleep, but after her night of wonderful lovemaking with Ethan, she'd had the best night's sleep she'd had in the past five years. The sun was starting to rise. She saw the lightening sky out the window. If she didn't hurry, all the MacKeefes would be awake and she'd have no chance to go back to the isle without someone seeing her leave.

Glancing over at the spot next to her in the bed, she could see the lump of Ethan's body under the covers. Sneaking out of bed, she looked for the dog, but it was still dark in the hut and she couldn't see it without lighting a candle – which she wasn't about to do.

Wishing for her own clothes, she had no idea where they were. So she had to don the MacKeefe plaid again that Ethan had stripped from her body last night and threw on the floor. Hopefully, Diarmad and the smugglers would all be gone with the shipment before she returned and she'd have time to change into some of her own clothes before anyone saw her.

That brought up another problem. She had no idea what

she would tell them about Isobel when they discovered her missing. Well, at least she might have a little time to talk things over with Kirstine before they returned. Diarmad and his men always left before the sun rose. The weather seemed to be clear so she could only pray they were gone. Together with Kirstine and Finn, she hoped they could come up with some kind of plan.

After dressing, she noticed her necklace in the bed and went back to get it, putting it around her neck. Then she donned a cloak, pulling the hood over her head, looking back at the bed in the semi-darkness one more time. "I love ye, Ethan," she whispered, feeling tears welling up in her eyes as her emotions almost choked her. She wanted more than anything to stay here and marry him like he'd planned, but it wasn't going to happen. Not now anyway. She had too much of a mess to clean up first. She had to come up with a plan and was finding it very difficult to think straight right now.

Hurrying out the door, she headed for the boat as fast as she could, constantly looking over her shoulder, hoping not to be noticed. It didn't feel right not saying goodbye to Isobel, but if she did, her daughter wouldn't want her to leave. She had to stick to the plan.

Thankfully, it had stopped raining and it looked to be a promising day. But since there was no wind, it might create a problem trying to sail back to the isle. She'd have to row, and that would take twice as long. Her body ached in a good way from making love with Ethan, but it would hurt like hell after rowing all the way back to the castle.

She broke through the trees where she left her boat, stopping dead in her tracks when she saw Ethan sitting in his own boat with his dog and also her daughter.

"Guid mornin', sunshine," Ethan called out. "We were startin' to wonder if ye were goin' to sleep all day."

"Ethan!" she exclaimed, realizing now why she hadn't seen the dog in the hut. And that bump under the blankets was naught but a means to trick her so she'd think he was still in bed.

"Hello, Mama," said Isobel, holding up a new rag doll that Alana had never seen before. "Look what Da gave me."

"What?" Her heart about stilled when Isobel called Ethan Da. "Ethan, how could ye have told her without even waitin' for me?" She stormed up to the boat.

"Now, calm down, Lanny. It's no' what ye think. She decided to call me Da on her own since she told me she didna have a da and really wanted one."

"Oh," said Alana, feeling terrible now. She never even knew that her daughter wanted a father. Then again, she supposed she had never asked. "Ye made her a doll?"

"Aye." Ethan smiled proudly. "I made it out of one of my auld leines and a frayed plaid. I didna want her cryin' durin' our trip back to the castle."

"*Our* trip?" she asked. "I dinna recall askin' ye to come with me. As a matter of fact, I dinna recall even mentionin' to ye at all that I was leavin'."

"Nay. Ye seem to have forgotten to mention that part. But I figured ye'd be here bright and early, so I took the liberty of meetin' ye here . . . with our daughter."

"Nay, Ethan. Isobel and ye are no' comin' back to the castle with me."

"Mama? Ye arena goin' to leave me here without ye, are ye?" asked the little girl about breaking Alana's heart. "I want ye, me, and Da to stay together from now on."

"I ken, sweetheart. I want that, too," she said and then let out a frustrated breath. This was going to ruin all her plans.

"Ethan, can I talk to ye privately for a moment?" she asked, pacing back and forth in front of the boat.

"Of course," he said, hopping out of the boat right into the water and sloshing his way up the bank. Trapper barked from the boat, looking like he was about to jump over the side. "Stay there and watch Isobel, Trapper," commanded Ethan. The dog whined and lay down on the seat with its nose between its paws. "Is there a problem, Lanny?"

"Is there a problem?" she repeated, angry with him, but trying not to show it for the sake of her daughter. "Ethan," she said in a low voice. "I dinna want ye and Isobel to go to the isle with me. How dare ye pack her up in the boat without even discussin' this with me first."

"Well, I couldna discuss it, since ye conveniently forgot to mention yer plans to me last night. I figured ye'd be off and runnin' again, and this time, sweetheart, I am no' goin' to let ye go without me. Without us," he said, looking back at Isobel who was making her doll talk, shaking it in the dog's face. Trapper kept his nose down and looked up at the doll with wide eyes but didn't move. It was so cute that it made it even harder for Alana to even think of leaving her daughter . . . or Ethan behind. Even if it was only to protect them.

Alana sighed. "Fine," she said. "Ye can take us to the isle but then ye'll need to return here. Ye canna stay at the castle."

"That seems like an odd arrangement for a husband to leave his wife and child unprotected. Nay, I canna do that," he refused, shaking his head.

"Husband?" Her head snapped up and she looked directly

into his eyes. "Ethan, I had a wonderful time with ye last night, but we are no' married."

"Yet," he said, looking up over her head to the bank and waving his hand in the air. "Over here, Faither."

"Faither?" she asked, thinking at first he was talking about his father, Onyx. That is, until she turned around and saw a small entourage headed down to the lake. Caleb led the group, holding his pine marten in his arms. Behind him was Logan and his wolf, and also Hawke, Storm, Lady Wren, Phoebe, and of all things, a priest! Apollo, Hawke's red tail hawk made lazy circles in the sky above them. "Ethan? What's goin' on?" she asked, feeling a bit panicked.

"One thing ye may have forgotten is that the MacKeefes are early risers. I figure it's best we get married before we even leave for the castle. That way, my friends can be here as witnesses. I had Caleb ride to a neighborin' village to fetch the priest before the sun even rose."

"We're – we're goin' to get married?" She could feel her heart beating in her throat. "Here? Now?"

"That's right," he said. "I figured it's the right thing to do since we've already had a child together. I dinna want anyone callin' my child a bastard."

"But . . . but . . ."

"Guid mornin'," Phoebe called out, waving her hand in the air from the hill. She held on to a bouquet of flowers. "It's a wonderful day for a weddin'."

"Ethan, how could ye?" Alana spat, feeling so out of control. She had plans but now everything was about to change thanks to him.

"How could I?" He chuckled in a sarcastic manner. "I think the real question here is how could ye leave me at the altar and then never tell me I have a child? I'll no' let ye get away again, leavin' me standin' here feelin' like a fool. Now, we're goin' to get married and ye have nothin' to say about it."

"But I canna marry ye. No' now. No' here."

"Why no'?" he asked, throwing down the challenge for her to give him an answer. "If ye have a reason, then tell me now. If no', then I suggest ye smile and act like ye are enjoyin' this, because everyone is watchin'. Alana, I'll no' let anythin' ruin my weddin' day . . . again."

"Are we ready?" asked the priest, stepping in front of them with his prayer book in his hand.

"Just a moment, Father Lewis," said Ethan, squinting in the rising sun and looking up the hill. "We are waitin' for a few more people to arrive first."

"More?" gasped Alana. "Ethan, did ye really have to invite the entire MacKeefe Clan?"

"Nay, I didna want to embarrass ye, so I didna do that," he answered. "But I asked the chronicler and his daughter to record our weddin' in the Highland Chronicles for our king."

"Ye did?" Alana was ready to faint. Ethan had made sure there was no turning back this time. He'd gone to extremes and there was nothing she could do but go through with the marriage as planned. It was what she really wanted in her heart, but now it was going to be even harder to figure out what to do once she got back and had to face Diarmad.

"Isobel," called out little Sophie, running down the hill to the lake, holding on to the hand of her brother, Oliver.

"Sophie! Look at my new doll." Isobel jumped up in the boat, rocking it and leaning over the side, almost falling into the water. Trapper gripped the back of her dress in his teeth and pulled her back into the boat.

"Guid job, boy," said Ethan, running over to the boat. "But I think I'll hold on to Isobel for now." He scooped her up in his arms and she clung to him, wrapping her arms around his neck, hugging him tightly. It was such a sweet sight that it about melted Alana's heart.

"Ethan, if we're goin' to do this, let's get started," said Storm. "I havena even had my mornin' ale yet."

"Storm was never a morning person," Wren said in apology. She grabbed her husband's arm and smiled at him. "Don't worry, sweetheart. I got up early and made haggis to give to Ethan to take back to the castle. I saved a little for you, too."

"Haggis?" Storm suddenly perked up. Haggis was one of his favorite foods.

"Are we finally ready now?" asked the priest impatiently. "I have another weddin' to perform this mornin' and I canna stay long."

"We're ready," said Ethan, holding Isobel in one arm and wrapping his other arm around Alana.

"Wait! Here is yer weddin' bouquet," said Phoebe, handing her a bouquet that Alana realized wasn't flowers at all. Since it was winter, Phoebe had used some hearty herbs of thyme, mint and sage.

"Thank ye," said Alana with a smile, taking the herbal bouquet from her, inhaling a big sniff of its powerful aroma. "If we get hungry later, we can eat it."

"Enough clishmaclaver," said the priest. "If we dinna hurry I'm goin' to miss the next weddin', so I'm goin' to make this fast. Ethan MacKeefe, do ye take . . . what's yer name, lass?"

"Alana. Alana Chisholm," she told him.

"Do ye take Alana Chisholm for yer wife?"

"I do," said Ethan, looking over at Alana and winking. He

looked so sexy standing there. And with little Isobel balanced on one hip, she could see he would make a great father.

"And ye, Alana Chisholm," continued the priest. "Do ye take Ethan MacKeefe for yer husband?"

Alana suddenly felt as though she couldn't speak. Looking out at the crowd, every single person was staring at her. Of course she wanted to be married to Ethan, but part of her felt it wasn't right to do so before she told him why she left him on their wedding day the first time. She really didn't know how to tell him she was being held captive along with her family and forced to help run a smuggling ring. Nay, it wouldn't be a good time to mention it. Perhaps she should have said something about it last night instead. But now it was too late. Part of her was also frightened to be married, because she didn't feel she deserved someone as good as Ethan MacKeefe.

"This is the part where ye say I do," said Ethan in a low voice. Still, Alana couldn't seem to say a word. Ethan leaned over and whispered into her ear. "If ye dinna say it, we'll stand here all day until ye do and ye'll never get back to yer castle."

"Nay!" she spat, glaring into his eyes.

"Nay?" asked the priest. "Ye willna marry him?" He slapped his book shut and let out a breath. "Why was I woken from a sound sleep and dragged here in the cold if this weddin' is no' goin' to take place?"

"It will take place, Faither," Ethan told him. "I'm sure Alana didna mean that in the way ye thought. Did ye, sweetheart?" he asked, making a big show of reaching up and kissing Isobel on the cheek while looking at Alana all the time, subtly reminding her he was the father of her child. He played a dirty game and Alana didn't like it. Then again, she supposed she couldn't blame him.

"All right," she whispered and looked back at the priest. "I do," she answered. "I will marry Ethan MacKeefe and be his wife."

"Yay!" shouted little Sophie, throwing her doll up in the air.

"Now the ring, please," said the priest.

"Give me the ring, Alana. I want to put it on yer finger," said Ethan. His palm shot out as he waited for it. Then he put Isobel down and untied Alana's necklace himself, slipping the ring and the key off the string. Alana reached out and took the key and string back, sticking them into her pocket. "Hold out yer hand," he told her.

Nervously, she held out one shaking hand and Ethan slid the ring onto her finger. She stood staring at it, not able to believe she was now his wife. She'd thought he was dead all these years, and now – now they'd finally said their vows and became man and wife. She was so overwhelmed she couldn't speak and once again felt like crying since this is what she wanted for as long as she could remember. To be married to Ethan MacKeefe. All thoughts of Diarmad, her father, and her horrible life were brushed away as she reveled in the good feeling. It was a dream come true. She smiled.

"Congratulations," said Hawke, coming to shake Ethan's hand. "None of us thought this day would ever happen."

"How do ye spell Chisholm?" asked Bridget, walking up with her father holding the Highland Chronicles in his hands. "I want – I mean, we want to make sure to spell yer name right for the king. Even though we dinna ken ye, I'm sure King Robert kens the Chisholms well."

"Aye," answered Alana, thinking how well they'd be known once her father was exposed for running a smuggling ring. She was sure his execution would be mentioned in that book as well.

"I'll spell it for them," Lady Wren told them. "Here, take this basket of haggis and bannock bread. I also put in some apple tarts and a few sweetmeats since Isobel seems to like them. There is enough there for your sister and brother as well, and even your father, too."

"Oh, thank ye," said Alana, taking the basket from Lady Wren. Her heart ached to stay here with the MacKeefes. Not all of them seemed to forgive her yet for leaving Ethan at the altar the first time but, still, there were quite a few of them who were welcoming her with open arms and that made her feel like part of the clan – part of the family. Even so, who was she fooling? She was far from being a true family with Ethan or anyone other than her family of cutthroat thieves back on the isle.

"Well, I guess it's time we get goin'," said Caleb. "I'll hold the basket." Slipping his pine marten into his pouch he took the basket from Alana. "I hope there's a little extra food in here for me and Slink as well." He lifted the covering on the basket to see, but Ethan's hand shot out and slapped him.

"Ouch," said Caleb. "What was that for?"

"I dinna want ye holdin' the food or it'll be gone before we make it to the isle. Here, take Isobel and get in the boat. I'll hold the basket."

Ethan picked up and handed the little girl to Caleb, switching with the basket of food.

"That smells so guid, and I havena had a bite to break the

fast yet since I was the one who had to fetch the priest in the dark," Caleb told him.

"Stop complainin'," grumbled Ethan. "At least I'm allowin' ye to come with us."

"Allowin'? Ye ordered me to come with ye because ye are afraid of goin' to the haunted castle alone." Caleb grumbled some more and carried Isobel down to the water.

"He's comin', too?" asked Alana, thinking things were getting worse. "Why?"

"Dinna fash yerself. He willna cause a problem," Ethan assured her. "And I promise I willna let him get anywhere near this basket of food." Ethan lifted the cloth and looked inside, and when he did, Alana couldn't help herself. She playfully slapped his hand the way he had done to Caleb.

"Ouch. What was that for?" he asked.

"Sorry," she said with a smile. "Ethan, ye're no' really afraid of a haunted castle, are ye?"

"Me?" He slapped his hand against his chest and cocked a half-grin. "Of course no'. I dinna believe in things like that."

Logan snuck up behind him, grabbing him by the shoulders. "Boo!" he said, making Ethan jump, almost dropping the basket.

"Ye fool!" said Ethan. "Do that again and I'll have yer head."

Everyone laughed and wished the newlywed couple well as they got into the boat and sailed away toward the Isle of Kerrera.

Alana was married now and hardly able to believe it. Everything was happening so fast that she hadn't had a minute to think things through. All she knew was that she was going to have to do something to get Ethan and Caleb to leave the isle before Diarmad and the others returned.

But now, it was going to be harder than ever. Because now, Ethan was not only her lover . . . he was her husband. Families were supposed to stick together, but she had a dilemma on her hands. She had two families now, and this situation was not the best. Once again, she was going to have to make a choice of what to do and she hoped, this time, it would be the right one.

CHAPTER 12

*E*than had figured Alana was going to try to leave him again, so he did the only thing he could to keep his newfound family together. He deceived her, just like she'd done to him.

He'd awakened early, making the bed look like he was still in it. Since she hadn't answered him last night when he talked about telling Isobel he was her father and also about getting married in the morning, that told him she didn't agree.

It was driving him crazy not knowing what she was keeping from him. Since she was so adamant about her secrets, he figured there was only one way he was going to find out anything. That's when he decided to go to the isle with her. Since he'd just discovered his new daughter, he didn't want to leave her behind, so he brought Isobel as well. Ethan had a family now and he would do anything he had to in order to protect them. He'd even go back to that bloody haunted castle – the last place he ever wanted to be.

The sail wasn't doing much since there was very little

wind today at all. Therefore, Caleb rowed the boat while Ethan sat back with little Isobel on his lap. She was so happy since he'd made her that rag doll that she wanted to be by him constantly – which he loved. Plus, the rest of the clan thanked him for it, too. Sophie had her doll back and wasn't constantly crying anymore. Everyone had a good night's sleep. Amazing how that worked.

"If ye'd like to row for awhile, I could use a break," complained Caleb. He eyed up the basket of food, which told Ethan he just wanted to eat.

"Nay, ye're doin' a fine job," Ethan answered, still sitting back, looking out over the water. "Besides, we're no' in a hurry."

"Ethan!" scolded Alana. "Is that the only reason you brought Caleb along? To row the boat?"

"Nay," said Ethan. "He's my friend. Friends do those kind of things for each other."

"Friends dinna let each other starve to death," Caleb answered softly.

"Well, I think Caleb deserves a break. I'll row for awhile," offered Alana, starting to get up off her seat to take the oars.

"Ye'll do no such thing." Ethan put Isobel down on the seat next to him. "Trade spots with me, Caleb, I'll row. With the rate ye're goin' we're never goin' to get there anyway. We both ken I'm much faster at it."

He didn't miss the smug look on Alana's face and wondered if she'd just tricked him into doing it. It didn't matter. Ethan never planned on having Caleb do all the work. He was only trying to keep him from eating all the food before they even stepped foot on the isle. Ethan removed his cloak and sat down, taking the oars and continuing to row.

. . .

ALANA'S EYES fastened to Ethan's arms. He'd pushed up his sleeves that only made his thick arms and bulging muscles more pronounced. She couldn't stop thinking about those arms and how he'd held her closely last night as they made love. She'd missed that. For five long years she'd been chaste, and now her sexual appetites were brought to life once again by the man she loved. Husband, she corrected her thoughts, suddenly remembering they were married now. She glanced down at her ring and smiled. She only wished her family could have been present at the wedding. Her mother would have been so happy.

Even though Ethan tricked her into it, she was glad he did. He'd made the decision for her. And now that she was his wife, she'd have to find a way to fix the wrongs of the past so she could live with Ethan and Isobel as a family like she'd always longed for.

"What are ye thinkin' about, Wife?" came Ethan's deep voice, causing her eyes to snap up from his arms to his face. She sat facing him as he rowed backwards. His dog lay at her feet. Caleb, Slink, and Isobel were behind him at the bow of the boat. Suddenly, the space closed in around her and she felt as if she couldn't breathe.

Her thoughts of Ethan's naked body pressed up against her, pumping into her as they both squealed in ecstasy was making her very randy. She had to look the other way before she started to blush or she'd give her thoughts away.

"I think my sister will be glad to see me," she said. "I'm sure, by now, she is wonderin' what happened to me and is very worried."

"I see," he said, sounding disappointed. "I had hoped ye'd say ye were thinkin' about us being married. Being husband and wife now."

"Oh, aye. That, too," she said nonchalantly, fussing with the clasp on her cloak, feeling her heart beating furiously because she was so excited by just the thought.

"Finn!" Isobel called out, gaining their attentions as they neared the shore of the Isle of Kerrera. Sure enough, there at the water's edge were Finn and Kirstine waiting for them. Finn was waving a hand over his head.

"Well, it seems someone is happy to see us," said Ethan. "However, I dinna see yer faither welcomin' ye home."

"Nay, he's too ill," she said.

"Where are the others? Like yer laird and his warriors?"

"Diarmad is Kirstine's husband," she told him. "He and his men are away tendin' to business. And they are no' warriors."

"Business? What kind of business?" he asked, making her feel very uncomfortable. "And if his men are no' warriors, what do they do?"

"Isobel, sit down before ye fall," she called out to her daughter, trying to change the subject.

"Fall?" Ethan jerked around in alarm, looking over his shoulder. "Caleb, hold her tightly. I dinna want my daughter to drown."

"Yer daughter?" Caleb grabbed a hold of Isobel. "What do ye mean?"

Ethan turned back around and looked at Alana as if he were asking permission.

"Well, ye might as well tell him now."

"Are ye sure?" he asked.

"Isobel," said Alana, causing the little girl to turn and look at her.

"Aye, Mama?"

"I never really told ye this, but yer da is Ethan."

"I ken," she said.

"Ye do?" she asked. "Did Ethan tell ye that?"

Ethan shook his head.

"Nay," she said. "But I told him he can be my da since I dinna have one."

"But he really is yer faither," she tried to explain to her daughter.

"Finn, look at my new doll," Isobel called out, more excited to show her toy to Finn than realizing Ethan was truly the man who sired her. "Her name is Olivia."

"Well, we tried," said Ethan with a shrug of his broad shoulders.

"So ye had a daughter and never told us?" asked Caleb, still trying to understand it all.

"I just found out myself," said Ethan, rowing the boat to the shore.

"Ooooh," said Caleb with a nod. Then his face became red as if he were embarrassed. He turned and waved at Kirstine and Finn on the shore. "Hello there," he called out. "It's just us again."

Alana and Ethan exchanged glances and he smiled, making her feel warm all the way down to her toes. She liked the fact he knew Isobel was his daughter and was happy that she'd told him. And although she fought it today, she also liked that she was married to him as well.

But there was a worry in her head that she couldn't shake.

She was sure her father, Diarmad, and the others wouldn't feel the same way when they found Ethan living at Blackbriar Castle with them.

Ethan docked and helped everyone to shore.

"Alana!" cried Kirstine, running to her and embracing her in a hug. "We were so worried about ye when ye didna return. We thought ye'd been drowned at sea in the storm."

"Nay, I am fine," she said, releasing her and looking over to Ethan who was taking Isobel from Caleb. Finn ran over to help them tie up the boat. Trapper jumped over the side and ran in circles on the shore as if he had too much stored up energy. "I stayed overnight at the MacKeefe camp because it was too dangerous to sail back with Isobel in the storm."

"I agree," said Kirstine. "But how dangerous was it stayin' the night with Ethan?" She smiled and waited for Alana's answer.

"More dangerous than ye can imagine," replied Alana, watching Ethan as he held Isobel nearly upside down while she reached out to pet the dog. She clutched her new doll like a lifeline and giggled.

"It seems like Ethan really likes Isobel," said Kirstine, watching them as well.

"Well, he should since he kens she's his daughter."

"Ye told him?" Her eyes opened wide.

"Aye, I finally did. And we made love afterwards, too."

"Ye did? Do tell."

"There isna much to tell."

"Och, it was no guid then?" Kirstine wrinkled her nose.

"Oh, nay, it was wonderful! What I mean is, I didna tell him about . . . about what goes on here."

"Well, that's understandable," said Kirstine. "And ye can never tell him. So, how long is he goin' to stay? After all, he needs to leave before Diarmad returns."

"He's . . . no' leavin' as far as I ken."

"But he has to leave, Alana!"

"Nay, no' really," she answered, wringing her hands in front of her, worrying about what to do. "Ye see, Ethan and I were married this mornin'. He is now my husband."

ETHAN WATCHED from the corners of his eyes as Alana talked with her sister. By the way Kirstine's mouth fell open, he was sure she'd told her they were now married.

"So, how long are we stayin'?" asked Caleb, walking up with the food basket over his arm.

"I'm no' sure," said Ethan, putting Isobel down.

"Isobel, come on, I want to show ye where one of the sheep got stuck in the fence and ate its way out," said Finn, taking the little girl by the hand. They ran off toward the stable together.

"Take Trapper and go with them," said Ethan, taking the basket from Caleb. "I dinna like this place. We need to keep a close eye on my daughter."

"Me?" Caleb made a face and looked back at the basket. "What about ye go and I'll guard the food." He reached out for the basket but Ethan moved it to his other hand.

"I'd go, but I have a feelin' I need to keep a close eye on my wife. There is no tellin' what we're goin' to encounter here, and I trust no one. Now, take Trapper and watch Isobel. I'll meet ye back at the castle."

"Fine," Caleb grumbled, pulling Slink out of his pouch and putting the pine marten on his shoulder. "But Slink and I are hungry, so ye'd better save a haggis or two for us."

"Dinna worry, ye willna starve. Trapper, go with Caleb," he told his dog.

The dog barked and took off at a run, following them.

Ethan strolled over to Alana and Kirstine who suddenly stopped talking when he got there. There were secrets going on again, he was sure of it. And, of course, he was not privy to them once again.

"Ladies, can I escort ye to the castle?" he asked with one arm outstretched for each of them although he was holding the basket.

"Congratulations on yer weddin'," said Kirstine. "I suppose ye two are plannin' on livin' back at the MacKeefe camp?"

"Well, I dinna ken," he answered as they walked. "That all depends."

"Depends?" asked Kirstine. "On what?"

"On whether or no' my wife is goin' to continue to lie to me, or tell me exactly what is goin' on at Blackbriar Castle."

"I'm sure I dinna ken what ye mean," answered Alana, exchanging a look with her sister.

"Well, then, I suppose that means we'll be livin' here," said Ethan. "Or at least until I can ask yer faither about what secrets are within the walls of Blackbriar Castle."

There was silence from both of the girls, telling Ethan exactly what he wanted to know. It seemed to him that Gil Chisholm was somehow involved in whatever deception was going on, and that made Ethan even more suspicious of everyone who resided at Blackbriar. Including the ghost!

* * *

TWO HOURS LATER, Alana was still acting like a nervous wreck since Ethan was at the castle. They sat in the great hall having finished off the basket of food that Lady Wren sent.

"Lady Wren makes some of the best haggis I've ever tasted," said Caleb, leaning back against the table, sitting with his legs outstretched in front of the fire. The great hall was nearly empty again and Ethan felt ill at ease. Was there really a laird named Diarmad and his men who lived here? He was starting to think not since he hadn't seen them yet.

"Ye like anythin' as long as it's food," said Ethan, pacing back and forth.

"Slink enjoyed it as well." Caleb looked over to his pine marten crawling around the top of the trestle table, eating any leftovers it could find. Trapper walked around sniffing the floor.

"Dinna ye think it's odd?" asked Ethan, glancing over at the girls across the great hall, still speaking in low voices to each other like a bunch of gossiping alewives.

"Nay, I didn't think it tasted odd at all." Caleb smacked his lips together and picked up a tankard of ale and took a swig.

"No' that, ye fool," said Ethan with a grunt. "I'm talkin' about the fact we've been here for hours and we've only seen a few guards and a handful of servants and still her faither has no' come to join us."

"That's fine with me," remarked Caleb with a yawn. "That means there will be more for me to eat. Besides, we dinna even like her faither."

"Somethin' is goin' on here and I intend on findin' out what it is."

"All right." Caleb yawned and stretched. "Let me ken what ye find out. I think I'll take a little snooze by the fire."

"I brought ye along to help me figure this out. Ye are turnin' out to be more of a hindrance than a help."

"I thought the reason ye brought me here was to do all the heavy work and rowin'."

"I'm goin' to take a walk around the courtyard and make my way up to the battlements. Now keep yer eyes open for anythin' suspicious."

"Will do," said Caleb, his eyes closing as he spoke. He leaned back against the table, resting his outstretched legs on a stool.

Ethan walked over and kicked the stool, causing Caleb's legs to fall.

"Blethers! What did ye do that for?"

"Why dinna ye take a walk to the other side of the isle and see what ye can find instead. I almost thought I saw the sail of a ship the last time we were here, but I could be mistaken."

"Walk to the other side of the isle? In the snow? Ethan, ye ken as well as I do that no ships even come near the other side of the Isle of Kerrera. The rocks are too jagged and there is nowhere to dock. Ye must have been imaginin' it."

"Perhaps," he said, knowing Caleb was probably right. "Come on, Trapper, mayhap ye'll be more help to me than Caleb. That is, if ye can sniff out somethin' besides food."

When he got to the door, Alana was standing there holding Isobel as she talked with Kirstine. Finn disappeared into the kitchen to talk with the few servants that were present.

"So . . . when exactly does everyone return?" he asked. "I'd like to meet this Diarmad who ye say is Laird of Blackbriar."

Kirstine and Alana exchanged worried glances.

"I think I'd better check and make sure Finn isna up to any trouble. Excuse me," said Kirstine, leaving them and heading for the kitchen.

"Alana, we need to talk," said Ethan.

"It's time for me to put Isobel down for a nap."

"Well, when ye're finished, I have some questions for ye, Wife. Questions that ye will no longer avoid. I want answers."

"Husband, ye are in my home now, and I will no' have ye demandin' anythin' from me." By the look on her face, there was no doubt he could have handled this in a manner that was a bit more subtle.

"We are married now, Alana," he reminded her. "A husband and wife should never have secrets from each other. Dinna ye agree?"

She hesitated for a second before answering. "Of course," she said, flashing a smile.

"Then tell me somethin'. What is this for and why were ye wearin' it around yer neck?" He pulled her key out from the sporran – small pouch – attached to his waist. He'd taken it from her pocket and she'd never even known it. But he'd needed to get a better look at it and he figured she'd never hand it over willingly. Holding it up by the string connected to it, he dangled it in front of her nose.

"My key!" she said in surprise, slapping at her chest as if she'd forgotten she no longer wore it and had put it in her pocket when they were married. "Give it to me." She reached out to grab it from him, but he quickly snatched it away.

"I'll hold on to this until ye put our daughter down for her nap. Dinna tarry, Wife. I'll be waitin' to talk with ye." He shoved the key back into his sporran.

"Excuse me," she said and left the great hall with Isobel in her arms.

"Well, I guess it's up to ye and me now, Trapper," he said, looking down at his dog. "Let's take a walk out in the court-yard and then up to the battlements and see what we can find."

CHAPTER 13

"Hurry, get in here," said Alana, pulling her sister into the chamber after she'd laid Isobel down for a nap.

"What are we goin' to do?" asked Kirstine. "Ethan canna stay here. It's too dangerous. Diarmad will return any day. And when he does, he will kill Ethan and Caleb."

"I ken," answered Alana, thinking now that this was a big mistake to let him bring her to the castle. "Plus, I'm no' sure Diarmad willna hurt us as well. Or Faither. However, I couldna stop Ethan from comin'."

"Well, ye're goin' to have to tell him somethin'." Kirstine groaned and laid a hand on her belly, making a face. "He is very suspicious and is walkin' around the courtyard as we speak. Albert said to tell ye to do yer thing and scare him away." Kirstine made another noise, rubbing her belly, holding on to the spindle of the bed for support.

"I can try," said Alana. "But it doesna feel right. After all, he is my husband."

"But it's for his own guid," she answered. "If he stays here he might get killed." This time, Kirstine started breathing heavily, and sat down on the edge of the bed, still rubbing her belly.

"Kirstine, what's the matter? Is it time for yer bairn to be born?"

"I dinna ken," she said, seeming worried. "I think it is too early yet, but I've been feelin' contractions."

"The time is gettin' closer. Yer bairn could be born any time now. Ye need to rest and stay off yer feet."

"Mayhap ye're right, Sister. I dinna want to lose another child."

"Ye stay here with Isobel. I'll play the part of the ghost again to scare away Ethan and Caleb, although I despise doin' it. I ken how frightened Ethan is of ghosts ever since he saw one as a child. It doesna seem right to use his weakness against him."

"It's for his own guid," Kirstine reminded her once again. "We have no choice but to do it."

"Finn will have to be sure to pick up the dummy as soon as I throw it out the tower window and scream. I dinna want Ethan to find it."

"I've already told him and he'll be waitin'." Kirstine moaned again.

"Ye need to lay down." Alana helped her sister lay down on the bed next to Isobel who was already sleeping. Then she walked around the bed and kissed her daughter on the head, tucking her in, thinking how much she looked like Ethan. Those same wide, brown, curious eyes and the little wave in her dark hair that Ethan had made it undeniable that he was her father. How could Ethan not have noticed the first time he set eyes on her?

Alana never liked playing the ghost because she was afraid somehow it was going to scare her daughter. But she'd explained to Isobel years ago that it was just a game. It didn't seem to bother Isobel and the girl could even sleep right through it now. But something was different lately. Isobel had seemed spooked at the castle, claiming she saw someone following her, and that someone was after her doll. She'd seemed so happy at the MacKeefe camp, but here, as soon as nightfall came, she was sure her daughter would be frightened again.

Alana couldn't blame her. Lately, this old castle seemed eerier than usual. And as much as Alana didn't like when her father's men were present, at least she didn't seem so spooked when they were near. Every time they went on a smuggling run, she felt frightened, thinking she saw someone in the shadows. She supposed it was her own mind playing tricks on her and hoped that was all it was. She needed to be strong and stay in control – and think with a level head.

Hurrying up the stairs to the vacant tower, she pulled the dummy stuffed with straw over to the window. It was in the shape of a woman, even wearing one of the white nightrails that Alana had found in a trunk that she supposed belonged to the last lady of the castle. That is, the bride who was killed by her husband. Horsehair was used for the fake ghost's hair.

"Ugh," she said, not liking to touch the thing. This was all her father and Diarmad's idea to keep people away from the isle. It had worked well this past year until Ethan and his friends decided to show up. "I hate this," she mumbled to herself, thinking she hated herself and her life as well. If only she could find the treasure her mother spoke of, mayhap things would be different. Then she could provide for her siblings and father if they were ever able to escape Diarmad. But now that Ethan had her key, that might never happen.

She hauled the dummy up to the window ledge, looking out into the courtyard but not seeing Ethan anywhere. Since Kirstine said he was out there, she figured he'd see this and hear the scream and get spooked and leave. She had no choice but to do it. Ethan was very superstitious, and especially wary of ghosts. She had no choice but to scare him away.

Hoping Finn was in position, she flipped the dummy out the tower window and let out a bloodcurdling scream, hating herself more than ever now.

Then she stepped back into the room with her heart thudding in her chest. Every time she looked out the tower window, she got a bad feeling. She wondered about that poor woman and how she must have felt going to her death. Then, from the corners of her eyes, she thought she saw the flash of white floating by in the room behind her. She spun around, holding on to the windowsill, but saw nothing or no one in the room.

"Nay," she said aloud. "It must just be my imagination."

Even so, it spooked her, and Alana ran from the room and down the stairs, wanting to be safe again in Ethan's arms.

ETHAN HAD WANDERED outside the castle walls with Trapper when, all of a sudden, he heard that awful scream again. His head popped up to see a woman falling from the tower and hitting the ground.

"The ghost," he said, his senses already on high alert. It didn't matter that he saw a ghost in broad daylight, it was still unsettling to him. All those emotions from his childhood surfaced and the hairs stood up on the back of his neck.

Trapper took off at a run toward the tower.

"Nay. Come back here, Trapper," he called out, running after his dog. When he made it to the spot just below the tower, he saw Trapper walking back to him with something big in his mouth. It resembled a person.

"What have ye got there?" asked Ethan, bending down to see it was a stuffed dummy made to look like a woman. "What the hell?" Suddenly things were starting to make sense. He realized he'd been made a fool of once again. There was no ghost at Blackbriar Castle. Someone was just trying to scare him away and he had a pretty good idea who was behind it all.

He heard the rustling of branches and turned to see Finn walk out of the thicket.

"Finn?" he asked, holding up the dummy. "Is this yer idea of a jest?" he asked through gritted teeth.

The boy stopped in his tracks and his eyes opened wide. "Nay," said the boy, looking frightened of Ethan. "I'm just here to pick it up. None of this was my idea at all."

"Alana," he growled. "She's purposely tryin' to scare me away, isna she?"

When the boy didn't answer, Ethan grabbed the back of Finn's cloak in one hand, still holding the dummy in the other and stormed back to the castle.

"I want an explanation for all of this," spat Ethan. "I want to ken what's goin' on here, and when I find out, someone is goin' to pay."

* * *

ALANA RUSHED DOWN THE STAIRS, meeting her sister coming up.

"Alana, what's the matter?" asked Kirstine. "Ye look like ye've seen a ghost." Kirstine suddenly realized the humor in the situation and started to giggle.

"I thought I told ye to rest," scolded Alana. "Why are ye climbin' stairs in yer condition?"

"I was restin' but I thought I saw someone walk by the door to the room and I came out to investigate."

"I think I saw the ghost, Kirstine," Alana blurted out, her body shaking. "It floated right by me up in the tower room."

"Slow down, Alana, I canna understand what ye mean. Did ye play yer part or no'? I thought I heard ye scream."

"I did. But afterwards, I swear I saw someone in the room behind me."

"That's impossible," said answered. "Finn is outside, Isobel is sleepin', and the two guards are on the battlements. Besides the few servants in the kitchen, it's only us here. There is no one else besides Caleb sleepin' in the great hall and Ethan who is out in the courtyard."

"Aye, but I ken what I saw. I'm tellin' ye there really is a ghost in this castle. I'm frightened. I need to find Ethan."

"Lookin' for me?" asked Ethan hauling Finn inside. Trapper led the way.

"Ethan!" cried Alana, running to him and throwing herself against him in a protective hug. "I'm frightened. There is a ghost in the tower."

"Oh, ye mean this one?" He pushed her away from him and held up the dummy.

"Och!" she cried. Her eyes immediately darted over to Finn.

"He got there before me. I'm sorry," said Finn, lifting his hands and shrugging his shoulders.

"I want an explanation," growled Ethan. "And dinna even think of lyin' because I ken ye have been actin' like a ghost tryin' to scare me away and I want to ken why. Now everyone, let's get to the great hall so we can discuss this at once."

They were turning to leave when another scream was heard from above stairs, and this time it wasn't Alana.

"That sounded like Isobel!" cried Alana, turning and running up the stairs with the rest of the entourage right behind her. "Isobel, are ye all right?" she cried, pushing open the chamber door to see her daughter sitting up on the bed clutching her doll and crying.

"I'm scared," said the little girl. Alana ran to her, but Ethan passed her up, getting to the bed first. He scooped her up in his arms and held her to his chest.

"Shhhh," he said, running a hand over her head. "Every-thin' is all right."

"I saw a ghost!" she said, sniffling.

"Nay, ye didna see a ghost," Ethan told her, looking over at Alana. "That was just yer mathair playin' a little game."

"Nay, it wasna. I saw it, too!" Kirstine said, rubbing her belly. "It was a man in a dark cloak."

"Nay, it wasna," said Alana. "It was a woman in a white gown."

"Alana," said Ethan, scowling at her. "Stop this nonsense. The game is up."

"Ethan, I admit I played the ghost, but this is different. This is real."

Isobel started crying and Ethan pulled her closer.

"Stop it. All of ye. Ye are scarin' Isobel. Now, I suggest we all go down to the great hall and discuss this." He kissed Isobel on the head. "Are ye all right, sweetheart?"

"Aye, Da," said the little girl, wiping a tear from her eye. "But I'm hungry."

Isobel surprised him by saying that and he chuckled. "Ye are startin' to sound like Caleb."

"Hungry?" asked Alana. "Sweetheart, we just ate."

"My daughter is a growin' lass and needs to eat," said Ethan. "I could go for a hot bowl of soup right now myself."

"Did I hear someone mention soup?" Caleb appeared at the door holding Slink. "What's all the noise about? It sure is hard to take a nap around here."

"We have a traitor in our midst," said Ethan, his glance shooting over to Alana.

"A traitor? What do ye mean?" asked Caleb with a yawn.

"I mean that my wife doesna want us here and will do anythin' to get us to leave."

"Nay, I do want ye here, Ethan," protested Alana. "I love ye."

"Well, if that is love, then I have a lot to learn," said Ethan. "Because to me, it seems that ye are nothin' but a big liar."

"I'm sorry, Ethan," said Alana, tears trailing down her cheeks. "I never wanted it to be this way between us, but I had no choice."

"We all have choices," he told her. "And ye chose to leave me and lie to me. I think it was a mistake to come here in the first place. I'm leavin' Alana. I'm leavin' and I'm takin' my daughter with me as soon as we eat and pack a few things for her."

He turned to go and Alana's heart felt as if she had a dagger sticking in it. "I canna live this way anymore," she said.

"Please stay, Ethan. Stay, and I promise I will tell ye everythin'."

"Alana, nay," begged Kirstine as Alana continued to cry. "Ye canna," she whispered.

"I have to," said Alana wiping her tears. "Kirstine, I refuse to keep livin' this way."

"What are ye sayin'?" asked Ethan, holding little Isobel to his chest and kissing the top of her head.

"We need to go to my faither's chamber," Alana told him. "Since he is a part of this, too, I think he should be present when I tell ye what's been goin' on for the past five years."

"Does this mean we're no' havin' soup?" asked Caleb, looking disappointed.

"Let's go," growled Ethan, scowling at Caleb. "But this is yer last chance, Alana. Ye either tell me everythin' or I swear I will take Isobel and leave and never return."

CHAPTER 14

"*A*lana? What's goin' on?" asked Gil Chisholm, sitting up in his bed as soon as they entered the room.

"Faither, we need to talk with ye." Alana led the procession into the room.

"Close the door, Caleb," commanded Ethan, walking over to a chair and sitting down, still holding his daughter. Isobel's little body trembled and he swore he wouldn't let her go as long as she was still frightened.

"All right," said Caleb, closing the door and walking back, holding his pet.

"Can I hold the weasel?" asked Finn anxiously.

"Finn, no' now," scolded Kirstine, sitting down on the edge of her father's bed.

"It's all right," said Caleb, handing his pet to Finn. "But Slink isna a weasel so dinna insult him. He's a pine marten. He likes to slink around."

Ethan cleared his throat. "If ye're quite done discussin' rodents, Alana has a lot of explainin' to do."

"Rodent?" Caleb reached out and covered his pet's head with his hand. "Dinna let Slink hear ye call him that!"

"Caleb," said Ethan in a stern voice.

"All right, all right, I'm sittin' down so we can discuss ghosts." Caleb looked around and plopped down on the floor next to Finn.

"What are ye doin' here?" asked Gil, jumping up, but being stopped by the chain around his leg that held him to the bed.

"I'm here with my wife and daughter, and I'm waitin' for answers," Ethan told him.

"Wife and daughter?" Gil's eyes darted over to Alana.

"Da, we were married today," Alana explained. "And Ethan kens Isobel is his daughter."

"Oh, Alana, nay." Her father sat down on the bed and buried his face in his hands. "This canna be. Do ye ken what kind of danger ye just put us all in?"

"I'd like to ken the answer to that. Go ahead and explain," Ethan told Alana.

Alana paced the room as she spoke.

"It all happened so fast," she told Ethan. "I wasna sure what to do. And I dinna ken where to start."

"Start at the beginnin'," said Ethan, holding Isobel to his chest and gently rubbing her back to calm her. "Tell me why ye left me at the altar. And then tell me why ye couldna take the time to find me and tell me I had a daughter."

Isobel laid her head against Ethan's chest, still holding tightly to the doll he'd made her, feeling very content in his arms.

"I – I had every intention of marryin' ye," Alana told him. "But I found out right before the weddin' from my faither's friend, Albert, that there was trouble. He told me my mathair had been abducted and that my faither needed me." She turned and held a hand out to include her siblings. "He needed all of us. He was in trouble and we had to leave Scotland right away. His life depended on it."

"Oh, we ken what kind of trouble yer faither caused with his thievin' ways," retorted Ethan.

"No' just with us. He caused a lot of trouble and I hear his own clan willna even welcome him back," added Caleb.

"Dinna talk about me as if I'm no' in the room," growled Gil. "And dinna blame my children for any of this. It is my fault that their mathair is dead and that Diarmad keeps us as prisoners and fearin' for our lives."

"Prisoners?" Ethan's body stiffened. He didn't like the sound of this at all. "So ye're tellin' me that Diarmad is real?" asked Ethan, surprised since he thought Alana had fabricated that story, too.

"Of course he is!" snapped Gil. "Who do ye think got my daughter pregnant?" Ethan's heart jumped, thinking he was talking about Alana, until the man nodded to Kirstine who groaned and looked like she was in pain.

"Och, I'm sorry," said Ethan, feeling bad for Kirstine but relieved that he didn't mean Alana. "So why is Diarmad holdin' ye as prisoners? Especially after all this time?"

"He's after the treasure," said Gil. "And he willna give up or set us free until he finds it. Meanwhile, he runs a smugglin' ring from the cove and forces us to be a part of it."

"A smugglin' ring?" asked Caleb.

"He's after treasure?" asked Ethan. "Alana, does this key have somethin' to do with this?" He pulled out the key and held it up. "Because I'm guessin' it isna the key to yer faither's shackle or ye would have used it by now."

"Aye," Alana answered with a sigh. "My mathair and uncle died to protect some hidden treasure, but I swear I dinna ken much about it, or where it is."

"It's right here in the castle, I tell ye," said her father. "It's here and we need to find it before Diarmad does."

"Alana, why didna ye tell me all this right away? If so, I would have handled it with the rest of the MacKeefes."

"That's exactly why," she told him, holding out her hands and shaking her head. "I dinna want ye or any of the MacKeefes involved. No one else will die over this."

Feeling agitated, angry, and ready to fight, Ethan put his daughter down on the chair and stood up with his hands balling up into fists. "I'll kill the men responsible for makin' ye live like this! I will kill every one of them to make them pay for what they've put ye through. And I'll start with yer faither." He took a step toward the bed with his hand on the hilt of his sword.

"Ethan, stop it!" cried Alana, grabbing him by the arm. "It was my choice to go with my faither. No one made me leave ye. Kill me if ye need to kill someone, because I am just as guilty as him."

Ethan paced the floor now, running a hand through his dark hair in thought. "What am I supposed to do with this information, Alana?" He stopped and looked at her and glared. "Ye purposely put yerself in danger, no' to mention ye've endangered my daughter, too. How could ye do such a thing? And how can I no' turn ye all in for what ye've been doin' here in secret? It's no' right."

"Isobel wasna even born when this all happened," spat Alana. "So I didna purposely put her in danger. I did what I had to do, Ethan. My faither's life was at stake. Wouldna ye have done the same thing?"

"Aye, calm down, Ethan," said Caleb jumping to his feet. Trapper got up and stood next to Ethan. "All that matters now is that we help Alana and her family."

"Well, if we're goin' to do somethin', we'd better hurry," said Kirstine, looking miserable, laying both hands on her belly now. "My husband will be returnin' any day now. And when he does, if he finds Ethan and Caleb here, he will kill them."

"Ethan, mayhap ye and Caleb should leave," said Alana. "Take Isobel with ye."

"And leave ye here?" Ethan let out a breath. "No' on yer life. Ye are my wife now and the last thing I would ever do is leave ye in the clutches of someone like Diarmad."

"Well, what are we goin' to do?" asked Caleb.

"Ye take the lassies and Finn back to the MacKeefe camp where they'll be safe," instructed Ethan. "When ye return, bring Logan and Hawke and anyone else who has forgiven Alana's faither enough to want to help."

"Ye're plannin' on goin' up against Diarmad and his men?" asked Gil.

"That's exactly what I plan to do. We'll capture them and also the smugglers and turn them in to the king."

"I'll help ye," said Gil, sitting up and rattling the chain on his shackles. "Help me out of this and I'll fight at yer side."

"Nay, I canna do that," said Ethan.

"Ethan? What are ye sayin'?" asked Alana. "Ye arena goin' to leave my faither in chains, are ye?"

"Alana, I'm sorry, but he has to pay for his mistakes. He's a thief and a smuggler and I canna allow him to go free."

"Let me loose," Gil tried to convince him, tugging on the

chain. "Help me out of this and I swear I'll help ye fight Diarmad. I'll even turn myself in when this is all over."

"Da, what are ye sayin'?" asked Alana.

"He's right," said Ethan. "He should turn himself in. It's the proper thing to do."

"Then I'm stayin' to fight off Diarmad, too." Alana crossed her arms over her chest. "And when this is over, I, too, will turn myself in for bein' a part of all this."

"Stop it, Alana. Ye ken ye arena guilty except by association with scum like him." Ethan's jaw clenched as he nodded at her father.

"I thought ye said ye were goin' to help me," said Alana.

"Ye, yes. Him, nay," answered Ethan.

"We are family," said Alana. "And family sticks together. Please, Ethan. Help us."

Ethan thought about it for a moment and finally nodded. "All right. I'll help ye and I'll even set yer faither free. But I swear, Gil Chisholm, if ye dinna turn yerself in and tell the truth that Alana and her siblin's had nothin' to do with this, I'll hunt ye down and kill ye myself."

"I told ye I would. Now get me out of this." Gil reached over and rattled the chain.

"It's against my better judgment and I'm sure I'll regret it, but I'm only doin' this for Alana." Ethan drew his sword and with one swipe, he managed to hit the lock. The shackle fell open and Gil quickly moved his leg.

"Bid the devil, ye nearly took off my leg," snapped Gil.

"Dinna complain. If ye're tried and convicted for smugglin', as well as all yer other crimes, ye'll be losin' more than just a limb."

"Enough of this talk." Alana rushed over and picked up her

daughter. "We probably have a full day, mayhap two before Diarmad returns, but no more. We've got a lot to do before then."

"We?" asked Ethan. "Ye mean I do. No' ye."

"Nay. If we're goin' to clear our names and, hopefully, the reputation of my faither, we're goin' to have to present more than just a few smugglers to the king."

"What do ye mean?" asked Ethan.

"Right after the meal, we'll start our search for the treasure."

"Alana, a little family treasure is no' goin' to sway even a king's decision," Ethan told her.

"Perhaps no'. But I think if we hand over the Templar treasure, we might have a little more to bargain with."

"Templar treasure?" gasped Caleb. "Like the Knights Templar?"

"That's the one," said Gil, rubbing his leg.

"Alana?" Ethan looked at her from the corners of his eyes. "Ye dinna say this is Templar treasure that ye are guardin'. That is a whole different story."

"So, it might be a bigger bargainin' tool to secure my faither's future."

"Well . . . I suppose it would," answered Ethan. "But I'm no' sure our king or any king should own it. Many Templar knights died because of people who didna understand their purpose."

"So what are ye sayin'?" asked Alana. "There is a treasure here and ye dinna want to find it?"

"Ethan," said Caleb in a low voice. "Findin' a Templar treasure would surely get ye mentioned in the Highland Chronicles."

Ethan felt confused about all this, and needed to think before he acted. But either way, if there was a treasure in this castle, they could not leave before it was found.

"I'll keep this for now," said Ethan, looking at the key that had a small Templar cross engraved in the center. "First thing in the mornin', I'll start lookin' for the treasure with yer faither while Caleb takes the rest of ye back to the MacKeefe camp."

"I'm no' goin'," said Alana stubbornly. "The treasure has been guarded by my family for generations and I'll be the one to find it or it'll no' be found at all." She snatched the key away from him and left the room with her daughter, followed by Kirstine waddling behind her.

"Here's Slink," said Finn, handing Caleb the pine marten and rushing out of the room after them.

"What just happened?" asked Ethan, feeling very confused.

Gil started laughing. "Ye have a lot to learn about bein' married to my daughter, MacKeefe. But I'll tell ye right now that no Chisholm, laddie or lassie, is ever goin' to want to be told what to do."

CHAPTER 15

"So when, exactly, will Diarmad and the others return?" Ethan asked in a low voice as they ate their meal in the great hall. The only two guards that had been left behind, Albert and Graeme, were eating near the fire with the servants, far from the dais.

"It willna be for a day or two yet, I'm guessin'," said Alana, balancing Isobel on her lap as they ate. "No one kens for sure. Still, ye will need to be gone before they arrive or there is no tellin' what Diarmad and the others will do to ye."

"Alana," said Kirstine from next to her. "The guards are askin' when Ethan and Caleb will leave. Graeme wants to kill them now, but I've convinced him that they dinna want to harm us but help us instead."

"I understand their concern. It wouldna fare well for them if the men came back to find Ethan and Caleb here. I'm sure they are gettin' anxious."

"I'm surprised they havena already tried to kill us," said Ethan, taking a bite of food.

"Albert and Graeme will listen to me," said Gil, happy to be sitting at the dais instead of being chained to the bed. "Dinna worry about them. I'll handle it."

Caleb loaded a heaping helping of fish on his trencher and handed the platter to Ethan. "Here ye go, Ethan. I saved some for ye," he said.

Ethan's stomach turned just smelling the fish. "Ye ken I dinna eat fish. I hate it. Save me some of the food I like and get that stinkin' mess away from me." Ethan pushed Caleb's hand away.

"Well, if ye dinna want yer share, I'll give it to Slink." He started to give it to his pet that was sitting on the table, but Ethan grabbed the platter and put it on the floor instead.

"Trapper can have my share," he said.

"Yer dog eats fish?" asked Alana in surprise.

"In case ye havena noticed, my dog is huge," answered Ethan. "He'd eat one of those guards if I told him to."

"Dinna let yer doggy eat my dolly," said Isobel, looking at the dog right below her with frightened eyes.

"Dinna worry, Isobel. Trapper would never harm ye." Ethan reached out and ran his finger along the girl's cheek. Such a gentle, caring motion made Alana realize that she had done the right thing in telling Ethan about Isobel. He would do anything to protect his daughter and that made her sigh in relief.

"So what's the plan?" asked Caleb, ripping off a hunk of his trencher and gnawing on it.

"The plan stays the same," said Ethan, finding meat and root vegetables on another platter and loading them onto his trencher. "Gil and I will search for the treasure and wait for Diarmad and the others to return."

"I'll talk to Albert, Graeme, and the servants," Gil told

Ethan and Caleb. "I'm sure I can convince them to work with us against Diarmad now that ye two are here."

"Caleb will be leavin' with the lassies and the children at dawn," Ethan reminded him, biting into his food.

"Och, Ethan, I want to stay and help look for treasure," said Caleb.

"Nay. I need ye to protect the lassies and Finn and bring back some of the MacKeefes with ye. We are goin' to put an end to all this."

"I dinna want to go back with the lassies," protested Finn, overhearing them as he walked by. "I'm a man now and want to help with findin' treasure and fightin' off smugglers."

"Finn, ye need to listen to Ethan," said Alana. "Besides, Isobel will feel more at ease if ye are with her since I'll be here."

Ethan groaned. He could see there was no use telling Alana she wasn't staying. Like Gil said, she didn't like to be told what to do. He supposed he shouldn't try to fight it.

"If ye insist on stayin' then we'll start searchin' for the treasure as soon as we are finished with the meal," Ethan told her.

"Where are we goin' to start lookin'?" asked Finn anxiously. "Mayhap the treasure is down by the cove."

"I'll help ye look there," offered Caleb, throwing his crust of bread to Trapper and brushing his hands together. "Let's leave now before the sun goes down." He jumped to his feet.

"Wait, I'll go with ye," said Gil, pushing up from the table.

"Nay, Faither, ye are too weak to go down to the cove," remarked Alana.

"Daughter, I'll take a horse if I have to. But nothin' is goin' to stop me from findin' this treasure, because I am doin' it for ye and Finn and Kirstine. Even for little Isobel and Kirstine's unborn bairn. I want to make certain ye are taken care of for the rest of yer lives since I willna be here to do it."

"Da, dinna say that," said Kirstine, looking very pale. "We've already lost Mathair and we willna lose ye, too." She put down her goblet and held her stomach. "Please, stay here. I might need ye since I am no' feelin' well."

"All right. I'll search the castle for the treasure instead," agreed her father.

Ethan was shocked by the way Alana's family had chosen to stick together, no matter what happened. He admired that. It also made him feel a little left out since he'd grown up never knowing his father until he was already a man. Ethan was naught but the result of a tryst between two young people experimenting in the act of lovemaking. This had made him feel unwanted through the years. He looked over to his young daughter, feeling sad he'd missed out on so much of her life, but also feeling blessed because he would be here for her as she grew up. He wouldn't give this up for anything. It meant more to him than any treasure.

"I'll start searchin' for what the key opens, startin' in the tower," said Ethan. He held out his hand to Alana. "Give me the key."

Her head snapped up and she slowly swallowed, licking the crumbs off her lips with her tongue, about driving him mad. All he could think about was kissing her right now.

"I'll go with ye," she said.

"Me, too," added Kirstine, trying to get up from the table, and then sitting back down. "Och, I dinna feel too guid."

"Really?" Alana rushed over to her sister. "Are ye still feeling cramps?" she asked.

"Aye. I think the baby wants to get out."

ELIZABETH ROSE

"It's too early," said Alana. "Ye need to rest so nothin' happens to this one, Sister."

"Mayhap ye're right. I think I'll go to our chamber and lie down."

"I'll take ye and Isobel there," offered Alana.

"Nay, Mama," said Isobel. "I dinna want to go to our chamber. That scary man comes out of the wall. He is tryin' to get Olivia."

"Ye're just imaginin' things, Isobel," Ethan told her. "There is no scary man and neither is there anythin' to be afraid of. Now, stay with Kirstine because she might need ye. Yer cousin will be born soon, and ye are goin' to have to help with the bairn."

"Me?" Isobel's eyes opened wide.

"Ye'll be the big sister in a way," he chuckled. "Do ye think ye can do it?"

"As long as Olivia can help, too," she said, kissing her rag doll on the cheek.

"Olivia can help, too," said Alana, taking Isobel by the hand. "Ethan, I'll meet ye in the tower. But why do ye want to start there?"

"It's just a hunch," he said. "Since that is where the lassie died, I figured somethin' else might have happened there many years ago."

"That's where I saw the ghost," whispered Alana, trying not to scare Isobel.

Ethan chuckled. "Enough with the ghost stories. Ye arena goin' to scare me off. Ye are the only ghost around here." Ethan started across the great hall with Trapper leading the way. As he headed to the tower, thoughts filled his head of the time he was a child and frightened out of his mind by what happened there.

Ten-year-old Ethan climbed out of the small boat with the burning torch gripped tightly in his hand. He eyed up the gloomy Blackbriar Castle that stood enshrouded in a thick fog in the night. His friends waited for him in the boat. As soon as he'd stepped foot on the Isle of Kerrera, he wished he hadn't been so gullible as to be tricked into coming here because he could already feel it in his bones that this was a big mistake.

"Go on, Ethan," his friend, Bram, coaxed him from the boat. "Or are ye a wench and too afraid to enter the castle?"

"I'm no' scared," retorted Ethan, really shaking in his boots but not wanting them to know. He'd heard the rumors of the crazy old man who lived here. Mad Murdock was a murderer, killing his bride on their wedding night, throwing her from the tower. Since that day so long ago, her bloodcurdling scream could be heard every night as she fell from the tower over and over again. In anger, the ghost of the bride of Murdock was said to walk the battlements in waiting, wanting revenge on the man who killed her.

"Remember, ye need to go all the way up to the tower and wave yer torch out the window so we ken ye are there," his other friend, Clyde, reminded him.

"I understand," he answered, looking at the castle and then back at them sitting safely in the boat. "Ye'll be watchin'. Right?" he asked, not wanting them to trick him and leave before he returned.

"Aye, of course we will," Bram assured him. "How else will we ken that ye really did it?"

"All right," said Ethan, taking a deep breath and heading up the hill. The night was so foggy that it was hard to even see the castle until he was upon it. He stopped just under the open gate, looking around. By the light of the moon, he saw the empty courtyard.

There, across the baily stood the infamous tower that was the scene of the murder. No one even knew that man's poor wife's name.

"I can do this," he said, feeling his body tremble. He'd heard the scream of the murdered woman just as everyone else in his clan had, the cry carrying on the wind all the way back to the mainland. All he had to do was to climb the spiral staircase and wave his torch out the window. Then his friends would see that he wasn't a milksop and they'd stop teasing him about being frightened of a ghost.

Wanting to get it over with as quickly as possible, he ran to the keep and down the corridor, using the light of his torch to guide the way. Tall shadows moved on the walls as he got to the foot of the spiral staircase, making him feel as if he were being watched. Or perhaps followed.

With a shaking hand, he held his torch in front of him, climbing the crumbling spiral stairs, wondering how far it was to the top. He stopped in front of the door to the room, looking back over his shoulder once more before slowly reaching out. But before he even touched the door, it creaked open on its own.

He froze. Was it the ghost of the bride of Murdock? Or was it perhaps old Murdock himself who did that? Waving his torch back and forth, he called out to the empty room.

"I have fire," he said, as if that made a difference. "And I have a dagger, too." He reached down to his waist and plucked his dagger from his waist belt, holding that out in front of him with his other hand. "Did ye hear me?" he called out, hearing the echo of his own voice in the room. "Ye canna hurt me so dinna even try."

As he took a step into the room, he saw a bed near the window but, other than that, the room was empty. Something squeaked from behind him and he spun around, stabbing his dagger in the air and waving his torch wildly. A mouse disappeared into a crack in the stone wall next to what looked like an empty old hearth. He walked closer, using the fire to light the wall. "Odd," he said, not seeing a crack big enough for even a mouse where the rodent had disappeared. It must have gone into the hearth.

He turned back and headed for the window, his knees still quaking and his legs starting to feel as if they were going to give out. "Wave the torch," he repeated the directions aloud, walking up to the open window to do it and leave. But just as he approached the window, a huge gust of cold air blew in, extinguishing the flame.

"Nay!" he cried, because now he'd never be able to signal to his friends that he truly was here. He turned around quickly, meaning to run, when a wispy form of a woman went right through him, taking his breath away. She floated out the window, and once again he heard that bloodcurdling scream. "Bid the devil!" he cried, running for the door. But when he got to the door, the dark image of a man in a cape stepped in front of him, holding up a halting hand.

"What are ye doin' here?" growled the man. His hand was so close to Ethan's face that Ethan could see the metal ring with etchings on it that the man wore. It looked to be some kind of cross on it. "Ye dinna belong here. What do ye want?"

"Get away from me," shouted Ethan, stabbing at the man with his dagger, still clutching the wooden torch in his hand. With one mighty blow, the dark image knocked Ethan's dagger from his hand and he heard his weapon sliding across the floor. Ethan used the torch to hit the man across the face.

"God's eyes!" spat the man, his hand going to his face. When he looked up, a beam of moonlight spilled into the room at that moment, illuminating the man's face as well as a section of the stone hearth behind him. "Ye drew bluid, lad. Ye'll pay for this."

Ethan saw the long gash above his eye. Blood trickled down his face. He drew his sword and Ethan realized it was time to run. He threw down the torch and darted out the door, nearly breaking his neck as he stumbled down the stairs in the dark. He ran as fast as he could back to the boat, where his friends were starting to row away without him.

"Wait!" he cried, sloshing through the cold water, throwing his body over the side of the boat. "Did ye hear the ghost?" he asked, his body shaking. "She floated right through me. And I saw a man who wanted to kill me. I think it was Mad Murdock. He was with me up in the tower room."

Clyde and Bram exchanged glances, looking shaken if he wasn't mistaken.

"Nay. Nay, we didna hear anythin'," said Bram.

"That's right," said Clyde. "There is no ghost."

"There is, I tell ye," he tried to convince them. "And I was up in the tower and I saw it all."

"Ye werena there," said Clyde. "If ye were, we would have seen yer torch in the window."

"That's right," added Bram. "Ye were too scared and turned around."

"Nay, that's no' true. I was there I tell ye, but the wind blew the torch out. I saw the ghost and I saw Mad Murdock. I was lucky to escape with my life."

"We dinna believe ye," said Clyde, rowing back to shore.

"Ye're just a whelp afraid of yer own shadow," said Bram.

"I thought ye were my friends," said Ethan. "Why dinna ye believe me?"

It was that day that Ethan realized he would never be free of his reputation. If his friends didn't even believe him, no one would. And from this day forward, he would never be able to shake the image of the ghost from his mind.

Pushing his thoughts of the past aside, Ethan climbed the spiral staircase leading up to the tower, taking the steps two at a time. There were a few torches lit in the corridors that cast eerie shadows on the walls, but he tried not to think of them as he made his way to the door and stopped at the threshold.

He drew his sword with one hand and with the other, he reached out and pushed open the door. That same bed was still there. It was probably the wedding bed that was used by Mad Murdock before he killed his bride. Swallowing deeply, he stepped into the room, looking one way and then the other. He had no torch in here, and the only light came from outside, through the one window.

He knew that window well. A shiver went up his spine as he remembered it clearly. He had actually felt a light pressure and a cold chill push through him that day as the ghost passed right through him.

"There is no ghost," he said out loud, for naught more than comfort since he was alone. "Alana fooled me. She was the ghost. That's all it was." He passed by the hearth and, once again, heard a scratching noise and a small squeak. He looked down and saw a mouse disappearing into that part of the wall. He took a step closer and when he did, a floorboard moved and lifted slightly. He bent down, pulling the board up, his hand going into the floor and his fingers closing around cold metal. He lifted out the object, realizing it was a dagger. Holding it closer, he saw that it was his dagger that he'd lost here when he was ten.

"My dagger!" he exclaimed, happy to have it again, but wondering how it got into the floor. He started to get up, but then the light from the window illuminated a spot on the hearth. It looked different in the light. It was getting late in the day and the light wasn't that strong but, still, he thought he saw an odd shadow. He took a step closer, reaching out for a brick that looked to be sticking out more than the others.

And right when he was about to touch it, he heard the bloodcurdling scream of a woman. He jumped back up to a standing position, spinning around with both hands gripped to the hilt of his sword, to find a dark figure standing in the doorway.

"Stay away or I'll kill ye. I swear I will," he commanded.

"Ethan? What's the matter with ye?" Alana hurried into the room, the last of the setting sun falling on her face.

"Alana?" he released the breath he'd been holding and slowly lowered his sword. "I dinna ken it was ye."

"Aye, I suppose no'," she said. "And next time, I guess I'll announce myself or risk ye takin' off my head. What is the matter with ye?"

"I'm sorry," he said, looking down and sheathing his sword. "I suppose I was a little spooked. I found my dagger that I lost here as a child." When he held it up to show it to her, once again came that bloodcurdling scream. "It's the ghost!" He ripped his sword from the scabbard, holding it with two hands and making a full circle as he scanned the room.

"God's toes, put that down before ye poke out my eye," said Alana.

"Didna ye hear that?" asked Ethan, half-expecting to see old Murdock coming at him with a blade. "It was the scream of the murdered lassie."

"That's no ghost!" spat Alana. "That is Kirstine havin' contractions." Ethan released a breath and sheathed his sword. "I came up here to tell ye the search for the treasure is goin' to have to wait. I think she is startin' to deliver her bairn, even though it is too early."

"Och," said Ethan, now feeling like a fool. "That's no' guid if it is too early."

"Exactly," she said. "My sister has already birthed a stillborn and lost two other unborn children. If she loses this one, too, I'm afraid she will go mad."

"We need to be there with her," he said, heading for the door. He had wished he could have been there for Alana when she'd birthed their baby. Family meant everything to him, just like it did to her. If he couldn't be there to support Alana, then he swore he would be there to help Kirstine birth her bairn instead.

He headed down the stairs, leaving Alana standing there.

"Hello?" said Alana, feeling like someone else was in the room. Ethan had left the tower, so no one should be there. "Is someone here?" she asked, not seeing anyone, but hearing a low whisper that gave her gooseflesh.

"Give up searchin' for the treasure," the male voice warned. "If ye dinna, ye will all die."

Frightened out of her mind, Alana bounded out of the room, following Ethan back to the solar.

CHAPTER 16

"*A*lana, help me," cried Kirstine when they entered the room. "I can feel the bairn comin'. Dinna leave me, please."

"Call for the healer," said Ethan, pushing into the room. "Oh, wait. Ye dinna have a healer. I dinna suppose ye have a midwife on hand?"

"Nay, we dinna," said Gil, hobbling back and forth. "We havena had one since we left Ireland.

"Then who is goin' to deliver the bairn?" asked Ethan.

"I guess we didna think about that," Alana answered, her thoughts still preoccupied by the voice she'd just heard in the tower room.

"Mama, I'm scared," said Isobel, running to her. Alana scooped her up in her arms.

"Well, now's a fine time to discover we have no one to help her," spat Ethan, rolling up his sleeves.

"What are ye doin' Ethan?" asked Alana.

"I'm goin' to help yer sister birth her bairn," said Ethan. "And ye are goin' to help me."

"Of course," she said, having planned on delivering the baby herself if she had to. But if Ethan wanted to help, so be it. She could use his support.

"Aaaaaah," screamed Kirstine, gripping at the bedcovers in the chamber she and Alana shared.

"I dinna want to see this. I canna watch," said Gil, heading to the door.

"Da, take Isobel down to the great hall," said Alana, handing her father his grandchild. "And send the servants up with boilin' water and lots of rags."

"Bring whisky, too," said Ethan, hurrying over to the bed. "Mountain Magic if you have it."

"Do ye think the whisky will help her pain?" asked Alana.

"I dinna ken," answered Ethan. "The whisky is for me. Gil – send someone down to the cove to get Caleb and Finn as well."

Trapper heard Caleb's name and started barking. Kirstine started screaming in pain again.

"Never mind," said Ethan. "Trapper, go get Caleb."

The dog continued to bark but didn't go.

"Go get Slink," he said this time and the dog's ears perked up. Then it turned and ran out the door.

"I'll be in the great hall if ye need me," said Gil, leaving with Isobel in his arms.

"Have ye ever done this before?" Alana asked Ethan.

"Nay. Have ye?"

"Nay." She shook her head. "But I'm sure it canna be that hard. Can it?"

"We'll find out," said Ethan. "We dinna have time to wait for those rags. Start tearin' up the bedsheet. And find a soft blanket to put the bairn in once its born. We need to keep it warm."

As Alana rushed around the room getting things ready, she smiled inwardly watching her husband. He was brave and jumped right in when family was in trouble. She loved him more than anything. This proved to her that she could always count on him. He would help her and her family be free of Diarmad and also clear their names. She didn't know how he'd do it, but she was sure he would. Now she wondered why she hadn't told him about her problem the first time she saw him.

"Alana," said Kirstine holding out her hand. "I dinna want my bairn to die. I dinna want to die either."

"Shhhh, Sister. Ye willna die."

"Oooooh," she cried out in pain, squeezing Alana's hand. "I will die, Alana. I do no' deserve to live, bein' Diarmad's wife. His child will die, too, because it should have never been. This bairn is unwanted."

"Haud yer wheesht!" said Ethan. "I willna hear talk like this again. I was an unwanted child, too. What ye need to remember is that the bairn had no choice in the matter. Ye need to be strong. Ye need to be strong for yer bairn, Kirstine. Dinna let this child live with guilt because it was born. It might be of that cur's seed, but dinna forget that the bairn is part of ye, too."

"Aye, he's right, Kirstine," said Alana. "Think of Mathair. She is watchin' ye and wants her grandchild to live. She loved children."

Kirstine sniffled. "Yer are right. Both of ye. I will be strong. For Mathair . . . for my bairn."

"Guid. Now that we have that settled," said Ethan, positioning himself at the foot of the bed, "I ask that ye forgive me for this, but just think of it as if I'm naught but a midwife." He flipped up her skirt and Kirstine and Alana exchanged glances.

"It's all right, Kirstine. Ethan would never do anythin' to hurt ye or yer bairn."

"That's right," said Ethan, examining the situation. "But I need to ask ye two to stop talkin' now. And Kirstine I need ye to push."

"Already?" asked Alana in shock.

"Alana, where is that blanket?" asked Ethan. "And I need those rags."

A HALF-HOUR LATER, Ethan's efforts were rewarded when he snipped the umbilical cord, holding Kirstine's little baby in his big hands.

"Ye've got yerself a fine lookin' daughter," he told Kirstine with a smile. The baby had trouble getting out but between Ethan and Alana, they did it.

"Kirstine, she is beautiful," cried Alana, taking the baby from Ethan, wiping it down and wrapping it in a blanket. The soft whimper of the newborn filled the room.

"Sister, is she really alive?" asked Kirstine, her body trembling.

"She is and so are ye," replied Alana. "Just like Ethan said."

"Let me hold her." Kirstine reached out and Alana handed the baby over to her.

"Yer sister will need to be cleaned up and she might need a few stitches," Ethan told Alana, feeling a wave of emotion and satisfaction surge through him. He walked over to the wash-basin and rinsed his hands as the servants stepped in to help Kirstine.

Looking back to the bed, he watched as Alana and Kirstine smiled, cooing over the baby. His heart went out to them. Was this the way it was when Alana birthed her baby? Had she felt scared and all alone? Ethan wished he could have been there for her.

Suddenly feeling the need to see his own daughter as well as to have a good swig of whisky to soothe his nerves, Ethan left the room and headed down to the great hall.

"Da!" cried little Isobel, running to him as soon as she saw him. He scooped her up, cradling her in his arms and kissing her on the head.

"Is the bairn here?" asked Finn, rushing over with Gil.

"Is my grandchild alive? Is it all right? How is my daugh-ter?" asked Gil sounding concerned as well as excited.

"Everyone is fine and Kirstine has birthed a wee girl," Ethan announced to everyone in the great hall.

"Can we see the bairn?" asked Finn.

"Go ahead," said Ethan. "But right now, all I want is some Mountain Magic."

"Here ye go," said Caleb, handing Ethan the bladder of Mountain Magic. "Did I hear right? Ye helped to birth the bairn?" he asked.

"I did," Ethan said, taking a swig of whisky.

"I want to see the bairn, too," said Isobel. "Put me down, Da."

He put her down and she ran to catch up with Gil and Finn.

"What did ye find down at the cove?" asked Ethan.

"No treasure if that's what ye mean." Caleb held out a piece of bread for Slink.

"It's no' there. It's up in the tower, I'm sure of it."

"How so?" asked Caleb.

"I remembered somethin' from my past. Somethin' I think I blocked out of my mind because I was so upset by what I saw when I was ten."

"The ghost?" Caleb picked up a tankard and took a swig of ale.

"No' just that. There was a man who guarded the treasure, I'm sure of it."

"A man? Who?"

"I'm willin' to bet it was Mad Murdock. And somethin' tells me that he is still here."

WHEN MORNING CAME, Ethan was headed for the tower before he even broke the fast.

"Ethan, where are ye goin'?" asked Alana, hurrying after him.

"To get the treasure. Do ye have the key?"

"I do," she said, following him to the tower.

"Guid, then ye can come with me."

Ethan's plan had been for Caleb to take the girls and Finn to the mainland. But now that Kirstine's baby was born, things had changed. Kirstine was in no condition to be riding across the water. Especially since today's weather changed for the worse. He also didn't feel good about bringing little Gavina out into the elements. Gavina is what Kirstine named her baby, after their mother.

"Mayhap it can wait until later," said Alana, sounding as if she were trying to stop him from going up to the tower. "Let's go break the fast first."

Ethan stopped and held out his open palm. "Give me the key," he said. "I ken where the treasure is hidden."

"Ye do? How can ye?" This seemed to pique her interest. She didn't hand the key over.

"I remembered something from when I was a child." He continued up the steps and Alana followed, both of them stopping just outside the door.

"Ethan, yesterday when I was in the tower I heard the voice of a man warnin' me to leave the treasure be. He said we would all be killed if we tried to take it."

"It was Mad Murdock," he said, pushing open the door and drawing his sword before he stepped inside. "He's guardin' the treasure. I realize that now."

"Mad Murdock? The murderer?" she asked, a shiver going up her spine.

"It all makes sense now, Alana. He is the one tryin' to scare us all away. I wouldna be surprised if there never was a bride who died. The more I think about it, mayhap I never even saw a ghost. He must have faked it, the same way ye've been doin'."

Just as he said that, Alana felt an icy shiver go up her spine. She was no longer sure about that. "Aye, I . . . guess so," said Alana, clinging to him so tightly, her fingers were digging into his arm. "I'm still a little scared."

"Dinna be afraid, lass," he said, pulling Alana into his arms and giving her a quick hug. He led Alana over to the hearth. "It's here," he said. "I ken it is."

"The treasure?" asked Alana. "Nay, I checked this tower many times and –" She stopped in midsentence, when Ethan pulled out a brick and then pulled open a secret door next to the hearth.

"Ethan! What is that?"

He reached into the enclosure, sliding out a large wooden box with a locked latch.

"I am willin' to bet we just found yer Templar treasure."

"Let me see," she said, kneeling down and running her hand along the carved wood. There was a Templar's cross on the box as well as symbols that she couldn't decipher.

"Open it," said Ethan, nodding at the box. "I want to see what's in it."

With a shaky hand, Alana pulled out the key that her mother had given her. She put it in the lock and slowly turned it until it clicked. "My mathair died to protect this treasure," she said. "So did my uncle. It must be very valuable."

"I'm sure it is."

She started to open it, but stopped. Somehow, she started thinking she didn't want to know what was inside. This treasure caused the deaths of not only people in her family but also so many of the Templar knights. "Ethan, I dinna think I can do it."

"Then let me," he said, pushing her hands out of the way and flipping up the lock.

"The box seems so small. I thought it would be bigger," she commented as Ethan lifted the lid and they peered inside.

"What's this?" growled Ethan, holding up what looked like a scroll.

"It seems there are only scrolls in here," said Alana in confusion, inspecting the inside of the box. "Ethan, are ye sure there is no' somethin' else in the secret hidin' spot?"

"Nay, that was it," he said, going back and checking for

possibly another hiding spot but he didn't find one. "There is nothin' else. Och, this doesna seem to be any kind of treasure at all."

"Oh, but it is," came a voice from behind them. Ethan jumped up with his sword in hand to come face to face with someone he hadn't seen in a long time now. The man had a long scar on his face by his eye and Ethan had been the one to give it to him.

"Mad Murdock," he spat, wanting nothing more than to run the man through with his sword. Because of this man, Ethan had lived his life in fear of ghosts.

"Step away from the treasure," said Murdock, holding out his sword.

ALANA SLOWLY STOOD UP, not able to believe there was a man in the room. "Where did ye come from?" asked Alana. "When did ye get here?"

"He's been here all the time," said Ethan. "My guess is that he's been scarin' everyone away because he is guardin' the treasure."

"Yer guess is right," said Murdock, taking a step closer. "I've been livin' in secret, Alana, since ye all claimed my castle as yers. There are many hidden passageways at Blackbriar. I've seen to it for a fast escape if I ever needed it."

"But I dinna understand," said Alana. "My mathair and uncle died to protect a treasure. Surely, it is more than just a few dozen scrolls?"

"The Templar treasure was split up, and hidden in many parts of several countries to keep it safe," explained the man. "Alana, ye dinna ken me, but yer great-grandfaither and mine were once guid friends, and also of the Knights Templar."

"What?" she asked in surprise. "But I thought they couldna have families."

"No' everythin' is always as it seems," he answered, keeping an eye on Ethan, as they both kept their swords raised.

"Ye see, it was up to our families to protect this part of the treasure. It was only supposed to stay here until another guardian came to get it. But as of yet, no one has ever come."

"I am no' surprised," said Ethan looking back at the box of scrolls. "I wouldna come for a few scrolls either. Are ye sure there is no' a box of silver or gold somewhere?"

"No' here," said Murdock. "And those scrolls are more valuable than ye think."

"What's on them?" asked Ethan. "The location of the rest of the treasure?"

"Nay," said Murdock with a chuckle. "It is solely religious and no' even in a language most of ye can read."

"Then what guid is this?" asked Ethan. "And why did ye kill yer wife over it?"

"I didna kill her!" shouted the man, making Alana jump.

"What about her ghost?" asked Alana. "Is that even real?"

"It is," he said with a nod, getting very choked up.

"It's said she wants vengeance on ye and that she walks the battlements and screams because she wants ye dead," said Ethan.

"Nay! That's no' true. She stays earthbound to protect me instead."

"I dinna understand," said Alana. "Why?"

"Because, someone came long ago to steal the treasure. She, just like yer family, Alana, died protectin' it. Actually, she died protectin' me. She jumped in front of a blade that was meant for me."

"Really," said Ethan. "What happened to the attacker?"

"There were more than one and I killed them all," said Murdock, getting a crazed look in his eyes.

"I willna let ye harm Alana and her family," snarled Ethan, once again wanting to take off the man's head.

"I dinna plan to. That is, unless ye try to take the treasure from me."

"We dinna want it," spat Ethan. "Take yer fool treasure and leave us alone."

"Aye, ye should have it," said Alana, closing up the box and putting the key on top of it. "Please take it and guard it. We mean no harm. We dinna want the treasure."

"Well I do," came a gruff voice from the door.

ALANA'S HEAD snapped up to Diarmad standing at the door with a half-dozen of his men right behind them. They were all armed and ready to fight.

"Diarmad," she cried. "Ye canna have this. It isna yers. It belongs to the Knights Templar."

"Step away from the box, Alana, or I swear I'll strike ye down dead," snarled Diarmad.

"Ye'll never have this treasure," shouted Murdock, swinging his sword at Diarmad. But Murdock was very old, and Alana wasn't even sure he had the strength in him to fight.

"I'm with ye, Murdock," said Ethan, lunging forward and taking out one of Diarmad's guards who had meant to kill him. With the clashing of swords, Alana's world once again felt as if it were crashing down around her. Murdock and Ethan could not fight off Diarmad and his men by themselves. They were going to be killed in the end.

"Nay! Stop the fightin'," she cried, but no one listened.

"Alana, take cover," shouted Ethan. "Protect yerself, lass."

"Nay. I want to help ye," she cried out, not even having a weapon.

"There is nothin' ye can do," he called out to her as four more guards entered the room and fought with Ethan and Murdock.

"Kill them. Kill them all," said Diarmad. "I'll get the treasure."

He came for the scrolls, but Alana couldn't let him have them. She picked up the metal box and backed away from him.

"Hand them over, Alana," snarled Diarmad. "Ye canna win. It's too late."

"Save the treasure," shouted Murdock.

"Enough out of ye," spat Diarmad, turning and shoving his sword into Murdock's chest. The man's eyes opened wide and his sword fell from his hand and clattered to the ground. Alana screamed. Now it was just Ethan to fight off everyone and the room was filling up with Diarmad's men quickly.

"Alana, I'm sorry," Ethan shouted. "I never meant for this to happen."

"I love ye, Ethan," she cried, knowing this would be their demise.

"I love ye, too. I never stopped lovin' ye, even when I thought ye left me."

"Enough of this doitit chatter," snarled Diarmad, giving

Alana a push, sending her to the ground. "I'll take that now," he said, bending over to pick up the chest.

Right as he did, a secret door in the wall opened and in ran Alana's father, and Caleb, Graeme and Albert and even Finn, all armed with weapons. Behind them followed the servants carrying pots, pans, pokers and eating knives, rushing forward into the room to help them fight.

Diarmad saw this and, holding the box under his arm, he pulled Alana to a standing position. He yanked her over to him and held his sword to her throat. Alana was so shocked that she couldn't move.

"Release her," spat Gil, moving forward with a dagger in one hand and his chain and shackle in the other. He limped since he was weak and ill.

"Alana!" shouted Ethan from across the room, fighting like a madman, making his way to her.

"Diarmad, ye have been a boil on my neck long enough," growled Gil. "Ye are responsible for the death of my wife and her brother, and for makin' my family live in hell all these years. I canna allow ye to live. Ye will die by my hand now, because I will gladly kill ye and have no remorse."

Diarmad chuckled. "Ye think ye can kill me, auld man, with just a dagger and a chain? Well think again."

Alana had to do something to help. So she stuck out her foot and tripped Diarmad, at the same time grabbing the treasure and diving to the floor. She looked up to see her father lunging at Diarmad. Diarmad raised his sword and Alana screamed as he stabbed her father. But her father did not give up. He hung on to Diarmad, pulling him to the tower window with him as he stumbled. Then in one motion, he pulled

Diarmad with him out the window and they disappeared as they plummeted to the ground.

"Nay! Faither!" Alana screamed, dropping the treasure and running to the window to look out.

"Diarmad's dead," Caleb called out, fighting with the rest of them.

"End this, now!" shouted Ethan. "Diarmad's men, listen to me. Ye are outnumbered. Surrender, and yer lives will be spared."

"Put down yer weapons," commanded one of Diarmad's men. They didn't do it, and continued fighting. Then Alana spun around when she heard the scream of a woman.

"It's the ghost!" shouted Finn.

Alana looked up to see a woman in white standing in the entrance of the secret passageway. Her head was covered and her arms waved wildly as she released a bloodcurdling scream once again.

"It's no' Alana," yelled one of Diarmad's men. "She's standin' right there."

"It really is the ghost," shouted another and, one by one, their swords hit the floor.

"We surrender," one of them called out and all the servants cheered.

Alana ran to the secret passageway, reaching out and pulling the veil from over the woman's head. "Kirstine!" she said and started laughing.

"I wanted to help, too," said her sister. "I'm glad ye're all right."

"Faither is dead," said Finn, coming over to his sisters.

"Where is Isobel?" asked Alana, suddenly frightened for her daughter.

"Dinna worry. She is in my chamber with the bairn," Kirstine told her. "Slink and Trapper are there, too."

"Take the prisoners and lock them in the dungeon until we decide what to do with them," commanded Ethan.

Hearing a moaning noise from the floor, Alana realized Murdock was not yet dead. She ran to him and dropped to her knees, using her tartan to try to stop the flow of blood from his chest.

"I'll help ye, Murdock. I'll sew ye up," she told him. "Dinna worry."

"Alana." He reached out and took her arm. "I'm about to die, and I need ye to keep the treasure safe now. Ye are the only one who can do it."

"Me?" Her heart jumped into her throat. "Nay, I dinna want to be the guardian. Please, dinna make me do it."

"Ye have to. If no', someone will turn in the treasure to the king. It canna fall into the wrong hands. These scrolls have valuable knowledge and belong to the Templars."

"So what am I supposed to do?"

"I have waited for years . . . but no one has come for it. Last night, I had a vision. Someone will be here . . . very soon. Ye will . . . ye will ken them by their ring. It looks like mine. Take it."

"Nay, I couldna," she said, looking at the ring with the Templar cross engraved upon it on his finger.

"Ye must. They will now . . . contact ye."

"What? How do ye ken that?" she asked. "They havena come for the treasure in all these years. Even with yer vision, how do ye ken it is true?"

"They will come," he said, his eyes closing. "It will be . . . soon. Now take . . . my ring."

She did as he asked, and then he smiled.

"Yer family would have . . . been proud of ye. Ye . . . helped to keep . . . the treasure . . . safe. And now . . . I can . . . die." With that, he closed his eyes and drew his last breath.

"Murdock? Murdock, please dinna die." Panic filled her. "Dinna put this responsibility on my shoulders." Tears streamed from her eyes. Then she felt a hand on her shoulder and looked up to see Ethan, bruised and bloodied but still alive.

"Come, Alana," he said. "I want to feel my wife in my arms to ken ye are still alive."

CHAPTER 17

$\mathcal{E}$than downed a swig of Mountain Magic, looking around the great hall of Blackbriar Castle the next morning, after having spent the night with Alana making love and holding each other all night long. The great hall was filled with people now, most of them being the MacKeefes who had come from the mainland at Ethan's request so they could decide what to do with the smugglers in the dungeon.

"Ethan!" called out a man.

Ethan turned to see his father, Onyx. "Da?" he asked, getting off the bench to greet him. "What are ye doin' here?" He embraced his father in a half-hug.

His father, although he was really English, was raised by the MacKeefes. Onyx ended up marrying an Englishwoman and lived in England, but he continued to act and dress like a Scot, never wanting to let go of the fact that he was a MacKeefe at heart.

"I was passin' through the Highlands, Son. Storm told me ye might be in trouble. What happened here?"

"Nothin' I couldna handle."

Onyx looked up with his two-toned eyes, one of orange and the other of black. "I hear ye're married now and ye have a daughter."

"Aye," he said with a smile. "I am married to my sweetheart from childhood, Alana Chisholm."

"Did I hear someone mention my name?" Alana walked up carrying Isobel. She looked vibrant today and almost seemed to glow since she was so relaxed and happy now that her family was free of Diarmad and they were no longer prisoners.

"Da, this is yer granddaughter, Isobel," said Ethan, taking the little girl from Alana.

"Well, hello there, Isobel. I'm yer grandda." Onyx smiled at the girl. She looked at his eyes and jerked backward, hiding her head against Ethan's chest.

"It's all right, sweetheart. Grandda's eyes are . . . different, but he is no' a demon," Ethan explained.

"Are ye sure?" she asked, peeking out, clutching her doll.

"I'm sure," said Ethan. "Now, I see Trapper over there and I think he is lookin' for ye. Why dinna ye take yer grandda over to see him?"

"Doggy," she said, no longer afraid. Ethan put her down and she took Onyx's hand and they headed away together.

"I am so happy that things turned out," said Alana with a smile. "But I do miss my faither."

"Alana, he gave his life protectin' ye and his family," said Ethan. "It was his choice. He chose to die rather than to have to be imprisoned or even tortured for his life of crime and past decisions."

"I ken," she said with a nod. "I suppose it is for the better. And as far as I'm concerned, he has redeemed himself. I will no longer think of him as anythin' but a hero – a man who died to save his family."

"I guess I can see that," said Ethan with a nod.

"Ethan, what will happen to me and my siblin's?" she asked. "Since we were involved in the smugglin' against our wills, I am frightened we will be punished in some way."

"Ye ken that the MacKeefes will do everythin' we can to clear yer names," said Ethan. "I promise I willna let anyone harm ye."

"Ethan," said Caleb, walking over with an older man who looked to be a knight. "This man says he is lookin' for Murdock."

"I'm sorry, but Murdock died yesterday," said Ethan. "Is there somethin' I can help ye with?"

"There wouldna happen to be anyone named . . . Chisholm here, is there?" asked the stranger.

"I'm a Chisholm," said Alana. "Or at least I was before I married Ethan. Now I'm a MacKeefe," she said, looking up and smiling at Ethan. "My name is Alana. Who are ye?"

"I'm Sir Douglas, and I am honored to meet ye," he said, reaching out to take her hand in his to kiss it. When he did, Alana gasped.

"What is it, sweetheart?" asked Ethan.

"The ring," she said softly, nodding at the man's hand. He wore a silver ring with a big circle and inside it was the engraving of a Templar cross.

"Aye, it was my great-grandfaither's ring," he said. "Does it . . . mean anythin' to ye?" He looked at her and waited.

She pulled Murdock's ring out of her pocket and held it up to him. "This belonged to a man named Murdock. Aye, it means somethin' to me."

Sir Douglas looked around quickly and then over to Ethan and Caleb. "Is there somewhere we can talk in private?"

"What for?" asked Caleb.

"I think ye have somethin' for me," said the man.

"Aye, right this way," said Alana, understanding now who he was. She led him up to the tower. Caleb and Ethan followed. When they were inside, the man looked around once more and then whispered.

"I have finally found ye. I am sorry it took so long. I have had others die and I have taken over their position of guardian but it has taken a while to find where to go. Now tell me, do ye have the Templar treasure?"

"Wait a minute," said Ethan. "How do we ken ye should really take it?"

"That's right," said Caleb. "Ethan, if ye turn that treasure in to the king, ye will get mentioned in the Highland Chronicles for sure."

"Alana?" asked Ethan. "Do ye think we can trust him?"

"Ethan, Murdock told me to look for the man with this same ring and to give him the treasure. Aye, we can trust it is him." She looked over to Sir Douglas. "Murdock had a vision and told me ye'd be here soon and he was right." Alana picked up the box with the scrolls and the key.

"Wait," said Ethan, as she started to hand it over. "Alana, if ye give that to the king, he will most likely clear yer name. Without it, I am no' sure what is goin' to happen."

"I dinna care," said Alana. "I have to do this. Too many people have died to keep it safe and in the hands of the Templars. I'll no' live with the burden of havin' made the wrong choice. My faither did, and look what happened because of it. Nay, Ethan. I need to do this. It is the right choice."

"I understand," said Ethan with a nod. "Ye are a special person, Alana. Go ahead."

"Well, I think she's daft," said Caleb with a puff of air from his mouth.

"Caleb, go wait downstairs," said Ethan, sending him away.

"Gladly," he said, and left the room.

"Take it," said Alana, handing Sir Douglas the box. "And use the secret tunnel to get back to yer ship so ye are no' stopped on the way out." She gave him the box and showed him to the tunnel.

"Thank ye, and God bless ye," said the man, ducking into the tunnel and hurrying away.

"That was a hard thing ye just did," said Ethan, pulling her into his arms after they closed the secret door.

"It wasna as hard as dyin' to protect it like my mathair or Murdock did," she answered. "I feel the weight of the world taken off my shoulders no' to have to guard the secret anymore."

"Ethan? Are ye up here?" someone called out.

Ethan turned to see his father. Storm, Hawke, Caleb and Logan entered the room with him. Trapper pushed through them, wagging his tail, coming to Ethan's side.

"What is it?" asked Ethan, doing nothing to move away from his wife. He kept hugging her as they spoke.

"Ethan, Storm tells me about Alana's predicament," said Onyx.

"She was involved in the smugglin' with her family, but they were prisoners and forced to do it," explained Ethan.

"We are takin' the prisoners from the dungeon to the king," said Logan. "He'll decide their punishment."

"What about my faither's friends, Albert and Graeme?" asked Alana.

"I'm sure if they tell the king where to find the rest of the smugglers, he'll give them a light sentence," said Storm. "They were involved with other things yer faither did so, for that, they will have to pay."

"Whatever happens to the smuggler, it's no' goin' to be pretty," said Caleb.

"Aye, the English and the Scots all want their heads," added Hawke.

"What's goin' to happen to Alana and her siblin's?" asked Ethan.

"Well, that's what I came up here to tell ye," said Onyx. "My sisters are guid friends with the Archbishop of Canterbury. I am sure if there are any problems on the English side, he will put in a guid word for Alana to their king. I'm sure it willna be a problem."

"Alana, as chieftain, I will personally allow ye and yer family to live with the MacKeefes," said Storm. "And I will vouch that ye and yer family were prisoners and were forced to be a part of the smugglin' against yer will. All the MacKeefes will vouch for ye."

"They will?" asked Alana, feeling blessed and truly part of the clan now.

"Aye, I'd do that," said Caleb.

"Us, too," Logan said, answering for him and Hawke.

"Aye," said Storm. "And the king likes us, so I wouldna worry. I also dinna think there will be any objections from the clan when they hear the whole story."

"I'd die to protect ye," said Ethan, kissing Alana atop the head.

"Oh, Ethan, I wanted to tell ye that Bridget and her faither are downstairs askin' a lot of questions," said Caleb.

"God's eyes, did they follow us here, too?" complained Ethan. "I suppose they have that book with them and are writin' some kind of nonsense in it as we speak."

"Ethan, that nonsense they are writin' is a lot of praise about ye," said Logan.

"That's right," agreed Hawke. "They are makin' ye out to look like some kind of hero for catchin' all these smugglers. Ye're gettin' a guid mention in the Highland Chronicles, dinna worry."

"What about the treasure?" asked Caleb. "Are they writin' about that, too?"

"What treasure?" asked Onyx.

Ethan cleared his throat and threw a warning glance at Caleb. "The only treasure here is the one I've found with my new wife," he said.

"Aye, I think that is all just a myth," said Storm with a knowing smile.

"Then I suggest we all get back to the MacKeefe camp and off this isle as fast as possible," said Onyx, looking back and forth.

"Why is that, Da?" asked Ethan.

"Because I've heard of the stories of the . . . ghost," he said. "And I, for one, dinna want to be around to see it."

"I think that is goin' to go into the records as just a myth as well," said Ethan.

"Really?" asked Hawke. "So ye're sayin' ye're no longer afraid of a little ol' ghost?"

"That's right," said Ethan, kissing Alana atop the head. "I'm no longer superstitious, so ye all can stop teasin' me about it now."

"Bid the devil, what's that?" Logan jumped and pointed over to the corner of the room.

"It l-looks like a ghost," said Hawke. His eyes opened wide as they all stared at the woman in white who floated up to the ceiling and then out the window. Trapper saw her, too, and started barking.

"What's the matter, men?" asked Ethan, no longer even shaken by seeing the spirit after everything he'd been through. Especially since he knew the ghost meant no harm but was rather a protector instead. "Are ye all afraid of ghosts now?" He broke out in laughter as they all turned and hightailed it out of the room with Trapper right behind them.

Alana and Ethan laughed, watching them go.

"So ye are really no' afraid of the ghost anymore?" Alana asked him. "That's wonderful."

"That's right," said Ethan, feeling calmer than he had in a long time now. "I'm over it," he said, kissing Alana on the lips. "Besides, I wouldna refer to her as a ghost after all."

"Nay?" she asked.

"Nay." He shook his head and smiled. "The way I see it, it's naught but a little *Highland Spirit*."

FROM THE AUTHOR

Thank you for reading Ethan and Alana's story in *Highland Spirit*. If you enjoyed it, I would love for you to leave a review for me.

I never meant for Alana to have so much sorrow in her life, it just kind of happened that way. But she was strong, and able to get through it. Especially with Ethan back at her side.

The relationship between Ethan and Alana was all about forgiveness and second chances. And it was not only about external conflict, but the inner battles they fought, too. For example, with Ethan's childhood memories and Alana's hesitance to tell him everything because of wanting to protect her family as well as to protect Ethan, too.

As this series continues, I must say I am becoming very fond of Caleb and can't wait to write his story. Caleb and Logan's stories are next, so be sure to watch for them in *Highland Spy* and *Highland Steel*.

The Highland Chronicles Series:
Highland Storm
Highland Spirit

Highland Spy
Highland Steel

When I first wrote the book, **Lady Renegade** – Book 2 of my **Legacy of the Blade Series**, featuring Storm MacKeefe, many years ago, I had no idea I'd someday be writing about the generations of the MacKeefe Clan. It is fun – and confusing at times – writing about the children of some of my more notable characters. The family tree is growing!

Thank you all for your support,

Elizabeth Rose

ABOUT ELIZABETH

Elizabeth Rose is a multi-published, bestselling author, writing medieval, historical, contemporary, paranormal, and western romance. Her books are available as EBooks, paperbacks, and audiobooks as well.

Her favorite characters in her works include dark, dangerous and tortured heroes, and feisty, independent heroines who know how to wield a sword. She loves writing 14th century medieval novels, and is well-known for her many series.

Her twelve-book small town contemporary series, Tarnished Saints, was inspired by incidents in her own life.

After being traditionally published, she started self-publishing, creating her own covers and book trailers on a dare from her two sons.

Elizabeth loves the outdoors. In the summertime, you can find her in her secret garden with her laptop, swinging in her hammock working on her next book. Elizabeth is a born storyteller and passionate about sharing her works with her readers.

Please visit her website at **Elizabethrosenovels.com** to read excerpts from any of her novels and get sneak peeks at covers of upcoming books. You can follow her on **Twitter, Facebook**, **Goodreads** or **BookBub.** Be sure to sign up for her

newsletter so you don't miss out on new releases or upcoming events.

Cowboys of the Old West Series

And more!

Please visit http://elizabethrosenovels.com

Elizabeth Rose